# The Woman Behind the Glass

By
Rose Elizabeth Kelly
Approximately 65,000 words.

Rose Elizabeth Kelly
RoseKellyAuthor@gmail.com

# Table of Contents

# Copyright

# Introduction

I knew I had something to say, and this is how I began to speak up. This book is entirely a work of fiction, however, we write what we know, embellishing and adding to the "what if."

The privately-owned painting, *The Woman Behind the Glass*, by Artist Nicolas Carone spoke to me partway through the first draft and completed the story. The paintings' owner, David N. Hart, Artist Nicolas Carone's eldest son, has given permission for the painting to be viewed on the cover and inside this novel. From my point of view, this painting has always been one of my favorite pieces.

You may think Rose' story is unique, unfortunately, it is not. If you take anything away from my book, please allow it to be this.

There are many stereotypes, but abuse isn't exclusively with the fist. Abuse doesn't discriminate and can happen to anyone, by anyone. It has no regard for gender, race, or population. An abuser may be a wife, adult child, sibling, friend, partner, parent, grandparent, and not only a man. Help is available for anyone willing to reach for it, so please reach for it. And don't forget at the end of every storm is a rainbow. Go find *your* rainbow.

*For my children, who make my life complete*

# Prologue

"Let go! Let go of my legs!" I screamed with all my might from the floor, but nothing I did seemed to stop him. Turning, I kick and I crawl, trying to grab anything to give me support. No traction can be obtained in my socked feet. My body is on an ice rink, as I fail to maintain balance.

I thought to myself, if only I could manage to crawl over to the door, I can anchor myself and get off the floor, and then I can run. Half turning, I draw my knee back and kick him, with the heel of my foot, in his back center mass. The stranger doesn't shift. "Get off me!" I scream until I'm hoarse.

Snarling, the sinuous man screams in rage as his sweaty hands wind up my prone body. His abominable strength overwhelms me as he flips me over and jumps on my hips with his weight, crushing my legs with his heaviness. I can't move. He clamps his huge meaty hand around my neck before he leaned forward extinguishing my air. I can't breathe. Instinctively I attempt to arch my back, making him lose stability, however, his body is too heavy to shift.

I fire my hand out to poke his throat, but he intercepts, rapidly slapping my arm off with his other hand. Spots began dotting my vision. I had to do something before he'll kill me this time. I scratch his face and poke his eyes with my fingers which made him howl in fury, and he leaned back with his hand still around my neck. Craning my neck up and to the left, I gasp a tiny pocket of air, I see him rear back his upper arm, fist formed, middle knuckle out. Using my last breath, I shake my head and beg, "Please! Please don't! Please! No!" Just before his fist makes contact he yells,

"Stupid bitch!"

I suddenly wake. Eyes wide open, covered in sweat, gasping for breath I sat up. I swear he was still in the room. I could smell him. His sweat clung to my skin instead of my own. My ears rang like cymbals and my heart remained pounding out of my chest. I wipe off my dejected tears from my dream. I can still recall his words like he was standing right by the bed screaming at me. His words were always the same. Having had that same dream for the last ten years, as history foretells, something was coming. What the hell is coming?

# Chapter One

I glanced at the alarm clock, as it flashed 5:15 am. I slept through my multiple cell phone alarms again. Getting out of the bed I stood, and stretched my fingers out from their locked fists, and stretched my neck muscles moving my head from shoulder to shoulder. Once my body was unfrozen, I began my grounding exercises.

Verbally, I recited my bad dream mantra and I spoke aloud, "The dream was not real, and I am safe. I must bring my mind out of the past into the present." I gaze around the room and begin.

"Mirror, dresser, nightstand, bed, blanket, smooth, grainy, smooth, firm, soft," I say. Two minutes later I finish my grounding exercises. Feeling more mindful, I opened the bedroom door and padded down the hall. After I let Pete into the laundry room to use his doggy door, I began my morning routine.

Already running late, after my speed shower, I put on my "Heavenly Ground" tee and my favorite jeans, hearing aid, and some light makeup. My flat-iron never failed with imperfect beach waves, as I pinned the left side of my hair back, I added my favorite blooming seashell rose hair flower. Once I turned to the mirror and placed my hands on my hips in a show of self-confidence. I looked at my reflection and began my daily affirmation. "Beautiful, Rose. Look at that sexy ass body. Full breasts, tiny waist, a rockin ass, and legs that go on for miles. I own that size 16! I might be forty-eight, but I've still got it!"

I'm allowed to feel positive about myself, though I'll never allow any man that close again. No matter how my libido tells me otherwise. I tried to be positive about my appearance, however, my frame never allowed me fit in. I was always taller, with a curvy figure. I stick out like a sore thumb on this island. Slight had not been added to the dictionary yet when God created me.

Walking into the kitchen I fed Pete, my American Bulldog, his morning breakfast then knelt to give him his scratches and daily words of affirmation. "My beautiful puppy love will keep our house safe all day, so I can come home and give my baby the biggest snuggles all night long. Pete, is going to have so much fun running outside, wee on everything, and chase that squirrel. Want pizza tonight?" Pete gave me a woof. I laughed and say, "Alright, alright, and as long as the salad is eaten first." I patted his butt and raised myself. I picked up my gym bag while setting the alarm as I got on my way. Today I will make a wonderful day.

#

Observing my surroundings covertly first, I got out of my old red SUV and walked in the back kitchen door of my cafe. I ambled to my office, dropped off my bags, and donned my logo apron from its wall hook. Kylie was here early and started the morning coffee, however, before I had the chance to indulge in mine, the back doorbell chimed. Perfect timing as always.

"I got it," I said to Kylie, as I round the corner, back to the kitchen. I open the back door plastered on my best fake smile and greeted John from the bakery. "Good Morning, John, come on in," I chimed.

"I bring yummy goodness," he says with his London accent. This skinny little pensioner, must have been born within the sound of Bow Bells. Thankfully, he says the same thing every day so I can understand him. When he says anything else, I just smile, nod, and answer, "OK". I think he knows I can't understand a word he says. I inspected as he unloaded our order to the bakery racks. With a brief nod, after signing for the delivery, I finish, "Thanks, John, have a great day," as I watched him go.

As a mostly deaf American in Belfast, working with the public gives me a run for my money. There were entirely too many accents in this town. Thank God for hearing aids or I would still work behind a desk. I choose to be proactive in making myself happy, and cubical bound, working alongside three thousand strangers is not my forte. Sure, my mind stayed fresh, but I needed the daily craic and banter of my customers to keep me smiling. Sometimes, with only a fake one. Someday, I will find my smile again, only I'm not sure how. My girls are grown, I'm independent and content, right?

I picked up the first tray of pastries, and cautiously walking out front, placed the tray inside the glass display case. After twelve trays, I poured myself my favorite Heavenly Brew, so I can start my day right.

Sitting in the back corner, I examine the whole cafe. Comfortable Sofas and coffee tables filled the space under the full glass windows in the cafe front. The eye-catcher, was the shiny long hardwood barista bar and glass sandwich deli, on the sidewall below the chalkboard menus. Quaint two and four-seater tables with antique iron footings graced the romantic theme, on the opposite side of the café, and the tables all include a small bouquet of fresh flowers. Claret walls adorned vintage color photos of romantic couples with the backdrop of the Emerald Isle. The polished concrete floor I had marble stained to accent the cafe's theme looked pristine. Customers will be coming in shortly, as I take a little personal time, preserving my harmony before the clamor begins.

#

Kylie had been running the till all day and made the hours breeze by. She understands every intricate order from every dialect like a pro. Not knowing better, I would say she was local and not American. Gabe and I managed the coffee machines and filled orders.

Friday is our most frenzied weekday and our patrons are always eager to begin their weekend, after getting to know so many of them, they seem like acquaintances now. We always smile and wave at each other outside the cafe. Occasionally, I listen to the craic and I joke with the best of them. I especially like petting their dogs when they sit outside under the awning at the bistro tables. They are the best. I wish I was allowed to invite them inside, but I always kept their water bowl full, and a tin of homemade dog treats.

Bending down to collect the next customer's muffin from the display case and heard his voice. When I looked up, I saw Liam. The most handsome man I had ever seen, at six foot four and thick brown hair that's a little too long, with some scattered gray in his well-trimmed beard. His oval-shaped face, prominent nose, and strong jawline oozed in masculinity. He has the biggest brown puppy dog eyes, and the broadest shoulders I had ever seen. The stature of the man, so strong and confident overtook the entire room.

He might appear menacing to some, with his slight limp and the scar that ran down the left side of his temple to his sculpted chin, which made him out to be a bad-ass male supermodel; but his pure soul shown through that tough exterior, exposing the kindest, most gentle man. To me, he was just a toasted marshmallow dreamboat. Hard and blistered on the outside and mouthwateringly gooey in the middle.

I knew he'd ordered the muffin, so he could watch me bend over. Kylie said he eyeballed me every time. The V-neck tee I wear may be the cause, but I refuse to wear crew necks. Anything that touches the front of my neck throws me into a panic. He never takes his eyes off me in the cafe if I hadn't been so infatuated with him, I would be unnerved, and most likely rude. He has always been the best part of my day. Well, that and the dogs.

I love it when he talks to me with that Scottish accent. The sound of his rolled R's makes me want to rub my hand down that big hunky hulk of a man's chest and purr. I may not be buying anything today, but a girl still likes to window-shop, and I liked what that store was selling.

Selecting the prettiest blueberry lemon filled muffin, I carefully placed the muffin in the paper bag. I prayed my body didn't betray me with my nervous rouge again, I finally stood, smiled, and chimed to my crush, "Hi, Handsome," as I felt the heat begin from my cheeks outward. I sensed the heat spread out my ears, and forehead, then down my chest. I began to perspire. How can one man affect my body this much?

I sauntered down to the end of the barista bar awaiting Gabe's delivery of Liam's white coffee. Drumming my fingers on the counter trying to remember how to breathe. Liam trailed not far behind me, knowing he was focusing on my back end.

Still heated, I took a deep breath gazed up at him, and asked, "How's Friday going, Handsome?" I had nicknames for all my customers. If they were new, I addressed them all as Honey or Sugar, like I would my kids when they were little. I think my customers appreciate the Americanisms I bring to the city center.

"Better, now that I've seen you," he says in that suggestive brogue. I nonchalantly wipe my overheated mouth in the hope I'm not drooling. Gabe sat the white coffee down in front of me with a significant grin, as I observed both he and Kylie were smiling in unison.

I ignored him, immediately sliding coffee to Liam. "Here's the muffin and coffee, Handsome. Don't work too hard, enjoy the weekend," I said with a nod to shift him out the door. I loved talking with him, but if he insists on licking the filling out of that muffin again; I might pass out right here. Someone, please dial 999!

He still hadn't taken his order off the bar, instead, he placed his palm on the counter and leaned toward me and spoke. Awe Lord, here it comes.

"Rosie, will you have supper with me tomorrow night?" Damn. How can I say no to this man? I recognized he was about to ask me to dinner when he leaned. It's always with the lean. I can't breathe. I can't look at him or anywhere. Frozen, I kept my head down as I stared at the counter. My phone saved the day as it vibrated, in my back pocket. Lifting my phone out, I glanced at my weekly reminder and turned off the alarm.

"S-H-I-T. Half five already. I'm late for my class. Later Liam."

"Aye, later Rosie," I hear him say, with clear disappointment in his voice as I dashed in the back to my office. After closing the door with my back, I tried to calm myself down with my breathing. Once the heat from my face and chest was gone, I was in control of my body again. I seize my gym bag and change for my class.

I don't know why he affects me the way he does. Men ask me out all the time and I turn them all down with ease. But with Liam, I was putty in his hands. More than anything, I want to have dinner with him, but I shouldn't. A relationship would be unfair to him with all of my baggage I carry around. Nobody should carry my crap bag but me, especially someone so nice. Quickly checking the security cameras on my desk to verify he had left the building, I collect my bags and head out to class. One step at a time, Rose. One step at a time.

\#

"Hi Pete, was my baby the best pooch?" I asked as I walked in the door and disabled the alarm. I was rapidly on my haunches covered in dog slobbers. How did I adopt the best dog ever? No accidents, nothing chewed up, and he was always happy to see me. Pete knocked me down to the floor and licked my face to the point where I had to stand up, and reset the alarm. He would eat me alive if I stay on the floor. Who needs a man when I have the best pooch in the world?

My self-defense course at Kerberos (Cerberus) was nearing an end. I asked Andrew, my instructor, if I could enroll in the next Close Quarters Battle Course they offered. The course strictly for their bodyguard students' and not available to the public, and chances were slim. He knew from the questionnaire I filled out in the beginning that I want to ward off an attacker at any given time. What else can I say, "Teach me how I can take somebody down in 3.2 seconds?" I won't share my violent history with an acquaintance. I keep that knowledge private from everyone but my best friends and immediate family.

Too many times I couldn't run away and that won't be repeated. Andrew and I had a remarkable rapport, and he says he would ask the Boss if he would allow me to take the course, but I won't hold my breath. I had never been strong enough to throw off a man, however, a woman I could. I had to be strong enough and no matter what I did, I was always overpowered by any man larger than me. Too many times I had tried and failed, so I did what I could by educating myself.

Over the past thirty years, I had taken three different types of self-defense courses. I had a state-of-the-art security system and safe room installed, and I adopted a big scary-looking pound puppy. Pete was trained to alert when he heard someone at the door, or something unusual in the house, or on the property.

I crafted one of the extra upstairs bedrooms into a workout room, as I had no need to leave the house for a crowded gym. Leaving my controlled safe zones was not my strong suit. My therapist, Lydia calls this "Social Anxiety" and taught me a mantra to say before I walk into a large store. She could call my anxiety anything she wants, but I say I need a going out partner. I could muddle through a smaller grocery store without glancing over my shoulder as much, but a big-box grocery store, gym, or mall forget it. Cybershopping was my favorite pastime. I only enter the huge grocery store or the mall if someone was with me. Usually, I opt for home delivery if I need anything from them, though.

Running was never going to happen even with a partner. I prefer listening to loud heavy metal music when I exercise. With my luck, I would be run over by a car. I might as well post a sign on my backside saying, "Aim Here." I couldn't hear if a cyclist or another runner was coming up on me. Recently, I preferred to keep myself at home, or at the shop. They are my controlled safe zones. I need to find my

fierceness again. It's still in there, I know it.

I slipped a frozen pizza in the oven and selected my

favorite dance playlist on my Bluetooth speaker. I had learned

long ago in the shelter about self-care. Every day, I had to

mind my mental health as well as my body. Dancing in the

kitchen with Pete, followed by a hot lavender bubble bath was

on the menu tonight. I needed to expel tonight's session out of

my head.

Andrew's forearm around the front of my neck tonight,

nearly threw me into a full-blown panic. Though he barely

touched the front of my throat, I had to breathe through the

anxiety. I had a significant number of flashbacks during the

exercise. I understand he was only demonstrating how to

remove myself from a sleeper hold, but when he touched the

front of my neck, my mind reverted where I can never go

again. Ages ago, I used to experience over three hundred

flashbacks a day, but I had been mindful of them and reduced them to less than ten. Now, I choose to live in the present, not the past.

After Pete and I shared our pizza and salad, I treated myself to a hot lavender bath, with my favorite hairband love songs. I could listen and sing badly to them forever. Exhausted and happily smelling like my Grandma, I went to bed with my tablet to read.

# Chapter Two

I awoke as Pete stood on my leg. "Pete, move. Your paws are hurting me," I slurred. I nudged him over with my other leg, but he whined and stood back up on both my legs and then growled. I had never known him to behave like that before. *Fuck.*

Wide awake now, I stare over to the closed door. My blood pressure skyrocketed, and all I heard my loud heartbeat in the darkness. Silently, I rose from the bed, and put on my bathrobe, pocketing my cell and hearing aid box as planned. Slinking in the moonlight shining through the curtain, I approached the full mirror mounted on the far wall. Quietly, I pressed the top two corners of the frame making thc false wall silently slide open. Next, I pressed in my access code to the digital keypad and the heavy safe room door opened.

Pivoting to the left, I and soundlessly unlocked the curtained sliding glass door and slowly slid it open partway. The intruder might think I fled through the glass door wall. My alarm didn't sound when I open the glass door. *Oh, God!*

Dashing into the safe room, I turned slamming my palm on the round red emergency close button. The door shut so abruptly my long hair took flight as I quickly counted my fingers. Thankfully, I still had all my digits. Once inside the entirely dark room, I felt around the side-wall, trying to recall where the light switch was. I hadn't been in here in ages. My creeping fingers found it and I switched on the lights. Dim red lights sluggishly illuminated the room as I noiselessly rolled the desk chair out of the way.

In the low-lighted room, leaning over the desk I switched on the four wall-mounted security monitors, one at a time. Slowly, the screens began illuminating, I turned on my hearing aid and snapped it on to my abutment. Thanking God, I had thought ahead and left a cheap pair of readers on the desk, I put them on and sat down.

Studying the first monitor, there was a man in the hallway, gradually opening my bedroom door, and I saw Pete. Oh! My God, Pete! I left Pete out in the bedroom! Watching Pete on the mute monitor, he barked like a rabid dog and lunged at the man repeatedly. Pete attacked, biting the man multiple times as pieces of the man's jacket flew everywhere. Quickly, I spun around and snatched the secure wall phone receiver and hit the speed dial for Kerberos. Turning up the volume, I sat and waited.

The operator answered rapidly as I whispered loudly, "Someone has broken into my house! My dog is attacking him and my alarm didn't go off!"

"Yes ma'am, you're calling from the secure Kerberos phone. Please state the answer to your security question, so I can get help to you," said the operator calmly with her English accent. I state my six-character word, "BITE ME".

"Thank you, ma'am and your name please for verification," she asked. With that Manchester, England accent, it sounds like she's addressing me as mom.

"Rose Kelly."

"Thank you, ma'am, a security team is being dispatched now. Where are you in the home," she asked.

"I'm in the safe room. This is the safe room secure phone. He is in my bedroom and OH MY GOD, HE JUST

HIT MY DOG! No Pete! No!" I covered my mouth with my hand to stifle my scream with tears running down my cheeks. *Shit! Shit! Shit!* I can't breathe and began to perspire with my heart was thundering out of control. Spots danced in my eyes, as I bent my body over, and hung my head between my legs hoping I didn't pass out. I threw off my bathrobe as the heat of my body claimed me. This can't be happening.

"Ma'am, a security team is nearby with an eta of five minutes. I alerted PSNI (Police Service Northern Ireland), and they will arrive as soon as they are available," she stated.

Swear to all that is Holy, five minutes, and he'll realize I'm in here, and I'll have to fight off yet another big man.

"Ma'am, are you still with me? Please stay on the call with me while you stay in the safe room," she said.

"Yes, I'm still here. Where the bloody hell do you think I need to go right now?" I bit out in repulsion.

"Ma'am, I understand your frustration, please stand by as I contact the security team directly," she said.

"Yep, no worries," I say. And stop calling me mom, Manchester.

Watching the monitors, Pete appeared to be wounded and hasn't moved on the floor. The intruder is standing at the glass door wall not four feet from me. I prayed he didn't realize I was so close to him or see the red lights. I really should keep my mouth shut. How was I so foolish?

Quickly, I flipped the light switch off, so the only light in the room was from the monitors. The intruder didn't seem to realize that there was a safe room because he didn't even turn to the mirror. Viewing the monitor patiently, he took two steps out of the glass door to the deck and shouted at someone back at the tree line. I sucked air in horror. "There is more than one! More than one! Do you hear me?" I pleaded to the operator.

"Yes, I am viewing of all your security cameras, ma'am. There are three individuals inside your home and one outside at the moment. Please wait for the security team. Ma'am, do you recognize the intruders," she calmly asked. Three more men! Everything is going to hell in a hand basket! How did I miss that!

I peered over at the other monitors and I observed one man in the back yard by the tree line, shouting at the intruder on the deck. One man, in the living room, was actively slicing open my £3,000 bespoke sofa with a long blade. A man was in one of the extra bedrooms upstairs actively throwing my daughters' keepsakes from the closet. The original intruder, that hurt Pete, stood just outside the safe-room door on the deck. I hadn't realized until now I've been holding my breath.

"Ma'am," the operator questioned.

"Yes, yes I'm here and no. No, I don't know them."

"Ma'am, as I advised before, it is imperative that you stay in the safe room until the premises is secure. Our security team will escort you out. I will communicate with you when it is safe to exit the room," she said.

"Okay. Like I said before, there is nowhere to go. They're everywhere."

Originally, I had the safe room built when I bought this house and, thought ahead. I had a bathroom installed, a sleeper sofa delivered, and enough food and water for three days. One thing I forgot to think of is more hearing aid batteries. My hearing aid just chimed, "battery low."

None of the body movements of the men look familiar. If only they took off their masks. Why did I keep attracting violent men? Do I wear a neon sign on my head that flashes ABUSE ME in red? Every time I had been assaulted, they said no one would believe me. Every time my house had been broken into I thought I was going crazy. Time after time my husband said it was my fault he was violent. It all added to my bank of "self-doubt." I will never be self-doubting again. No more! These men are on camera and I have evidence.

"Ma'am, the four intruders have exited the home and entered the tree-line behind the house. The security team would greet you on the other side, once the house has been cleared. Please stay in the safe room until you are advised otherwise," the operator announced.

Just sit and wait. I waited about three minutes, then viewed the entire front yard light up.

"Ma'am, the security team has arrived and are breaching the home now. Please stay in the safe room. I repeat, stay in the safe room."

Two men, in dark clothing, walked up to my front door and tried to open it. Is that Callum? Two more men walked around my lawn checking the shrubs and along the tree line in back. One of the men in front picked my lock faster than a locksmith. Callum and the other man both walked around the house separately. Weapons pointed in front of them, they cleared each room one at a time. I should've realized they would be armed. They both kept touching their left ear and speaking, even though they cleared separate rooms on separate floors. They must have communication devices. Both of them kept speaking intermittently, but without having audio on the cameras, I couldn't quite read their lips.

Then, I saw him. Liam walked up to my front door, scanning the area with his hand on his holstered sidearm, and his back to the door. He never had that in the café. Why the hell is he here? Oh, God. I blew him off and never gave him an answer for Saturday night. I can't worry about that now.

Liam waited on my front stoop for several minutes. He tapped his earpiece and spoke to someone or someone's several times. Callum walked out of the house to Liam, and said something. They both entered the foyer and walked to the kitchen, as they continued speaking to each other. Another man joined them in conversation after he walked down the stairs. Liam looked angered and barked something at Callum. How dare him. Callum had always been so kind. Never have I seen Liam him act like that. Callum didn't seem to mind, though, as his face lit up with a huge smile. I wish I knew what they said.

They walked back to my bedroom together. Liam stood for a moment overlooking Pete. Bending over, he checked my puppy for a pulse. Pete looked dead. My poor puppy looked dead. The last thing I said to him was in frustration. Pete was only trying to alert me. He was doing what he'd been trained to do. Callum had been in here and cleared it, but Liam still walked around the room, taking it in. Finally, after several long moments, Liam walked to my wall mirror and pressed the two top corners, opening the secret wall.

"Ma'am our security team is on the other side of the safe room. It is safe to exit, now." I hung up the phone and stood entering the exit code.

I ran out of the safe room past Liam's mistakenly open arms and knelt to Pete. His dead black eyes and mouth were open, and his body was lifeless. Under him was a stagnant pool of blood as I inspected him. Carefully lifting his head with my left hand, I felt around. Inching my fingers around his mangled head, I found his gash and his skull broken into pieces where the blood was pooling. My poor baby. I kept stroking him from his head to his butt repeatedly, but I knew

he was gone. Pete was my protector, my ears, and my best

friend. He didn't deserve this.

Tears pooled and I finally blinked to set them free.

Sobbing, I covered my face with my other hand in shame. I

didn't mean to leave him out here. Leaning down, I kissed his

cheek. Cradling his poor broken head, I whispered in his ear

and begged him to forgive me.

A monstrous hand brushed my shoulder. I had

forgotten the security men were in the bedroom with me. I

turned around and observe Liam looming over me. He held

out his palm saying,

"Come on Dearheart, let's get you out of here."

*Dearheart?* I haven't heard that term of endearment in years. The sound made me melt inside the way he rolled his R's. *Get a grip, Rose. He just yelled at Callum.*

I took his hand and stood. Wrapping his arm around my shoulders he led me out of the room, when I stopped saying,

"I need my batteries, mine chimed." Turning around when Liam released me, I finally took in the room. My top mattress was flipped halfway over, leaving my bedding on the floor. The tall dresser was moved out and all the drawers were empty on the floor. The wardrobe was open with my clothes and shoes strewn about haphazardly. My nightstand was intact, though. Opening the top drawer, I opened the small box of batteries, after wiping my bloody hand on my bathrobe, and snapped a new one in my small digital lifesaver. I also took my hair tie and pulled my hair into a ponytail.

Liam said something to the other man in the room, then led me down the hallway, and out to the kitchen, with his hand on the small of my back. We arrived in the kitchen, where all of my cupboards appeared to be open, and they had been rifled through. Some things lay on the floor, like my Grandmother's baking sheets and rolling pins.

My open floor plan allowed me to view the living room, from the kitchen. Just as I had seen on camera, the sofa cushions had been sliced open, as had the back and beneath the seating area. The sofa was flipped over and the lining was cut open underneath. The same pattern appeared with my cuddle chair and ottoman. The huge framed print on the wall was lying on the overturned coffee table, with the back removed, however, the small photos remained intact on the walls. I walked into the foyer and reception noticing the same pattern.

Walking upstairs, I viewed the same path of destruction as the first floor. After walking downstairs again, I entered the conservatory, which I called our music room. My baby grand had been propped open and the bench moved. My daughters' larger instrument cases were open, but nothing was removed. The smaller photos, hung on the walls untouched. *What were they looking for?*

I entered the kitchen and scrubbed my hands under the tap. I filled the kettle and switched it on to heat. Shock was beginning to set in and I needed my licorice peppermint tea to wake me up. Liam pulled out a chair and patted the seat adding,

"Let's have you sit down and we'll go over what we know, Aye?"

I took the seat and looked down at my hands. My brain was a mush of tangled seaweed as Liam began,

"Rosie, do you recognize any of those men tonight?"

Frustrated and angry, I continued to look down at my hands and replied, "No, even without their masks, I would probably say no too. Their movements didn't spark my memory."

"Before we view the video, do you know what they were looking for? With the destruction they did, they were looking for something, most likely sizable," he identified. I looked up at him and explained,

"I don't own anything of value other than my homes, and the cafe. I own some guilt jewelry my husband gave me that I saved for the girls, and a few hundred in cash in the safe, but they're all in the safe room, where I was."

"Aye, your TV is missing," Liam confirmed.

"I don't keep one downstairs. We keep a small one is upstairs in one of the closets for when the girls are home." The kettle button popped up, and I stood and continued making my tea. Taking the coffee and English tea from the cupboard, and a box of deluxe biscuits, I placed them on the counter for my guests. I haven't lost all my proper Irish manners, yet.

Two men walked in the front door. Liam stood as he introduced them, "Rosie, this is Callum and Ian, they work at Kerberos. They were the first on the scene and called me when your name appeared on the security alert. Declan and Matt will be in shortly, they are checking the tree line and field for tire tracks."

I gave a short smile and nod, "Lovely seeing you again, Callum, and Ian. The kettle is hot if you'd like a cup, and biscuits are there." I took my seat again, next to Liam. He pulled a laptop out of his computer bag, placing it on the table and booted it up.

"Rosie, let's go through the video, and prospect for identification of what they were after. I don't think they were after, you, though."

While Liam logged in, I turned to him whispering,

"I hadn't realized that you worked for Kerberos, Liam."

"I don't work for Kerberos, I own Kerberos. I wear all black tactical attire. I thought you knew, Rosie," Liam said.

"We've never discussed it. A lot of men dress like that at the cafe. So many, I never imagined you all worked together, but I never saw a sidearm," I said shaking my head. Liam smiled at that and started the video.

I viewed each camera feed until we reached my bedroom. Seeing Pete being struck, I broke down in tears. Liam rubbed my back to comfort me as I sobbed, but I had to continue before the Police Service arrived. Once we started

the final video I said, "Stop, back up." Liam did as I

requested. As the video played, I whispered to myself, "She's

not here. No. He's not here. No. It's not here. It's not here. He

said, it's not here."

"What's not here?" Liam furrowed his brow and said.

"I'm not sure, but that's what he said. I have to read

lips to help me understand what people are saying to me. Part

of my hearing loss is nerve deafness. I only hear part of the

spoken word. He wasn't looking for me. He said whatever he

was looking for was not here. He was looking for something

else. Whatever it is, they didn't find it. Could they be in the

wrong house?" Liam cut in,

"We'll have to figure out what "it" is then. They kept

shining their torches on the walls, checking the closets and under the beds, I agree, I don't think they were looking for you, either. Whatever they looked for is sizable."

Police Service Constables walked in the kitchen for their report then, and after I gave my statement it was 3 am. I stood in the kitchen, preparing to pack a few items for the Lough house, when Liam approached me stating,

"Rosie, I'd like to take you back to my house for the night, until we can make some headway on this. You aren't safe to stay here. Go ahead and grab your things. I'll wait for you."

"Thank you, Liam, but no. If I go anywhere, it will be at my house in Carlingford. No offense, it has a security system from another company, and I should be fine. I'll wrap up the dog and take him with me. I'll take him to my old vet down in town. He knows Pete."

"Rosie, I highly advise against that. It is not safe for you. Who's to say they didn't acquire knowledge of your other house and are already on their way? Who's to say they didn't break into that house first?"

"No one, but my family and close friends know about that house. I've kept it private under a shell company since I bought it, in the Republic, and with a different security company. *If* I arrive and there is any evidence of forced entry, I'll turn around and go to a hotel or stay with a girlfriend nearby. Give me your number and I'll call you tomorrow for an update, on how my alarm got hacked." Liam openly frustrated, shook his head and said,

"Rosie, I'm not alright with this," he argued in boldly.

"You don't have to be, Liam. This is my choice. No one is taking my decisions away from me. Thank you, but you've done your job. Go home and get some sleep. Leave your number on the table, please." I stated defiantly and walked to my bedroom closing the door with my back. Liam had his men wrap Pete up and place him in the garage earlier. They also cleaned the hardwood floor, which was kind of them. Immobile, I stood for the longest time as my sorrow slipped down my face.

I'm so tired of putting my life back together. I thought those days were over long ago. I guess I was wrong. Tonight, my twelve year old pound puppy paid the price with his life. I took a cleansing breath and began putting my life in place again.

After I shifted my top mattress back on the bed and remade it, I began hanging my clothes from the floor to the wardrobe. At least they were still on the hangers. I stuffed my clothing in my dresser minus what I was going to change into. After dressing and packing a few essentials in a duffel, I opened the bedroom door, duffel in hand, and walked down the hall to find Liam still at my kitchen table.

"Why are you still here, Liam?"

"Making sure you make it out in one piece. A few hours ago four men invaded your home and you're walking about like everything is fine. Everything is not fine, Rose." I ignored his statement and walked into the garage with my duffel, placing it in the front passenger seat of the SUV. He had followed me into the garage as my shadow. Bending over, I carefully picked up my wrapped dog off the cold cement floor. Liam stepped forward and held out his arms attempting to take him from me and saying,

"Let me handle this Rose, you don't have to do this alone."

"Let me carry my own dog one last time before his body seizes up, please! The vet will carry him in from the car in the morning." My voice cracked, and I started to cry again as I carried him to the trunk. Liam opened the trunk while I placed Pete inside and lovingly laid him to rest. I couldn't help but cry as I positioned my poor baby down and kissed him for the last time. Liam wrapped me in his arms and turned me to face him. Drenching his shirt, I let my tears free, while he rubbed my back. After a long while, he said,

"I'm so sorry, Rosie. Why won't you take my help?"

"I need to work this out on my own, Liam." He wouldn't let it go. I can't bring him into my shit storm of a life. He placed his hands on my upper arms and leaned back asking me with those big brown eyes in empathy,

"Why? I am here and I want to help you."

Ending the standoff, I finally and politely said, "Go home, Liam. Thank you for everything. I don't mean to sound ungrateful, but I am angry, because my dog is dead, and my house was nearly destroyed. I need to be on my own to work this out in my head. Please, I need this." He released me and nodded. I went inside, turned out the lights and locked up. I pulled out of the garage to see Liam was in his Rover waiting for me. After I gave a short nod and wave and drove to my Lough House in Carlingford. *Damn, his arms felt good.*

# Chapter Three

Wrapped in a blanket I sat on the sofa in the dimly lit house,

watching the sunrise over beautiful Carlingford Lough, as its

bay opened to The Irish Sea. The tide was getting ready to roll

out, and the sunrise bounced off the water; reflecting all of our

worldly selves back out to the heavens in adumbration. This

had always been our sanctuary. The place where we could rid

ourselves of our burdens and wipe the slate.

The Lough house was the first home I had bought for

the girls and me after we left Ciaran. All of our recent

milestones had been celebrated here. All of our good

memories shaped a loving family within these old stone walls

and in the front garden. I couldn't fathom anything happening

to our sanctuary. The thought of it overwhelms me, but I will not allow myself to be melancholy again. I overcame too much to revert to depression. After we left Ciaran, aside from the necessary activities, I slept for four months. My mind and body needed to recover, as it could not take any more malevolence.

Had Ciaran's past dealings' anything to do with the men broke into my home? No, it can't be. Any evidence was destroyed before we left the States, and he only had thumb drives left, and we burned those. This new intrusion doesn't feel right, and it certainly isn't their usual bullying behavior. We never had break-ins back in Chicago or here. Only physical warnings outside the home ever happened. They knew Ciaran had kept the girls and myself out of dealings. Having said that, if they wanted anything or to harm us, they would have done so years ago.

Pushing my sore body off the sofa, I walked to the kitchen and prepared the coffee pot. I could hear the bleat of my neighbors' ewes and adorable lambs in the background

waking up with the sunrise. After opening the pantry and

pulling out the shelf-stable milk, I poured myself a bowl of

muesli for breakfast.

As I leaned against the kitchen counter, I observed the

baby lambs being nursed by their mothers. I always loved

watching them. They were so innocent and fun-loving,

without a care in the world. They bounce around the meadow

around the ewes and other lambs. I love to toss the seeds to

them. They never approach me, but if I throw the nuts far

enough, they love them.

The neighbor's donkey heard me in the house. She was

waiting for me by the old stone wall. I hadn't brought any

fresh fruit for her today, so I'll need to pick some up later. I

don't dare approach the fence without any. Opal named her

Therese. By the looks of her, she's pregnant. Therese found

her white knight. I wonder what Opal will name the baby. Knowing her, it will be hysterical, probably Little Flower.

By the time I finished my bowl, the coffee was done. After pouring my first cup, I placed the now opened milk in the refrigerator. Walking back to the sofa, I continued my observance of this amazing sight. The seagulls weren't squawking around yet and the morning mist wouldn't start for at least another hour.

Sitting there, I wished Pete were with me, snuggled behind my legs, under the blanket and snoring. Closing my eyes I nestled into the throw pillow in the hope of catching a few moments of sleep. After nearly an hour, I gave up. Opening my eyes, I spotted about four of the neighbor's golden chickens pecking my front garden. They usually stroll through a few times a day. We're far enough off the main road, they don't wander far. They never walk up onto the deck, they stay strictly on the lawn. Thankfully, I didn't have to worry much about their droppings. I made a mental note to stop by and purchase some fresh eggs for the week. They had the best eggs around.

Pulling out the house tablet from the coffee table drawer, I turned it on. Checking the security camera app, I noticed Liam's rover parked by the garage. How long had he been here?

*Why doesn't this man give up?*

Slipping my tennis shoes on first, I entered the garage and opened the small side door. Strolling to his window I knocked. Startled from his slumber, he rolled down the window and said,

"Hey."

"Come inside Liam, the weather is too cold out here." Turning around, I stepped back into the garage, leaving the doors open for him to follow. Liam got out of his Rover and entered the house behind me.

"Want some coffee before we begin?"

"Aye," he said with a nod. After preparing him more of a coffee with milk than a white coffee, I handed him his cup, then held out my palm and invited him over to the sofa. Liam sat on the far end from me. After he had a few sips of his morning brew, we gazed at the serene waterfront together and I began.

"I used to live here with my girls after I left my husband. It was our home, and we always loved it here. As the girls each went away to University, I had to move forward and accomplish something with my life. I bought the cafe and the house on Black Mountain as I needed something to do to keep myself and my mind busy. One of my favorite things was watching the bay when the sun comes up. It centers me. Now,

I come here on the weekends to ground myself for the next week to come. This is what I do on Saturday nights and Sunday mornings. I sit here, on the porch swing, on the deck, or out in the garden and read by myself.

Liam peered own at his cup and nodded in contemplation. Hopefully, he wouldn't ask me to dinner again. My answer would be no, having confessed, I would rather spend my time with an inanimate object. It was a small white lie.

"How did you find me, Liam?" He gazed over at me and explained,

"I didn't find you, I followed you. It was quite easy, actually. You didn't lift your eyes once and look for tails."

"Why?"

"I needed to make sure you were alright. I wanted to make sure no-one else broke in and harmed you," he confessed.

Shaking my head, I turned away from him saying, "I appreciate that, but I am okay. Nothing is going to hurt me here. Only close friends and family have ever been here. That's why I bought it. I haven't received mail here in years." Liam furrowed his brows together in frustration and tried to change my mind, firmly stating,

"Four men invading your home and killing your dog, state otherwise, hen. If they're looking for something, they won't stop at an open border. I don't know what you thought a shell company would stop, but it won't stop them. These villages are so small, anyone could ask about the American woman, with red hair, and everyone would point to you. This was not a random attack, Rose. You were targeted. I don't believe the attacked the wrong house, either. They want something that you possess. I watched the video again, and they were outside on the tree line watching you for two hours before you turned out your bedroom light. There are no street cams since you live so far up Black Mountain, but something's not right."

Turning away and continued my view over the Lough. That last bit about them watching shook me, as the information was alarming. I wasn't far from speaking my mind. Nodding my head, with this new knowledge, I conceded, "I agree, something's not right, but I'm not sure what, and I was my natural blonde when I lived here, and changed the color when I moved." After a few moments, I knew I needed to remove myself from his presence so that I could think straight.

Without turning to him I said, "My mind won't stop running like a jackrabbit. I'm going to shower. There's more coffee in the pot if you want and plenty of food in the pantry if you're hungry. The guest bathroom is off the kitchen. Enjoy the view. The Lough is spectacular this time of the morning before the trawlers come out. Sometimes, you can even see dolphins." I stood and walked upstairs, not looking back.

After my shower, I changed clothes into one of my favorite V-neck tees from back home that comforted my soul. The back read, "Our Buns are Steamed." No one here would know what it meant, but I did and it's all that mattered to me. I strolled downstairs in hopes my Glaswegian had left. No such luck as Liam was still here, outside standing on the deck, sipping his coffee. Walking outside and toward him as he turned to me and said,

"This spot truly is spectacular, hen. When the tide's out, do you pick mussels?"

"A few times a year I indulge, but only when I'm in the mood. I steam them with Garlic and fresh herbs, then make a cream sauce with their liquor over pasta," I said smiling. He turned to me and smiled in return adding,

"Do you ever get oysters at the place down the road? They're supposed to be the best in all of Europe."

"No, my dad does when he's here. He and my mom like them raw. They're not my thing unless they're cooked. I mince them up and put them in my stuffing. Don't tell my kids, or they'll stop eating it, and it's one of their favorites," I admitted with a chuckle. My daughter Grace likes to fish off the pier. Occasionally, we'll throw lobster pots out if we're in the mood or have company. We try to stay near the shore, as we've lost several pairs of wellies during low tide. What a sight that was. Four women sucked into the sand with the tide coming in." I smiled in remembrance. "Liam, I saw you bark at Callum last night on the camera. He turned to you and smiled. You looked angry, though. What was that about?

Liam tried to suppress his grin and admitted, "He and Ian agreed it would be best if I met you at the safe room, since I like your coffee so much."

I laughed. No wonder he barked, he doesn't scare me, and he is still gooey Liam. I advised, "Liam, I'm taking Pete to my old vet, then driving to the Police Service in Belfast to see what they have. If you'd like, you can come with me, or we can talk later." Liam peered up at me, after a moment he nodded and finally said,

"I'm sure you'll be fine in both places. Watch for tails this time, please. I'll go home and shower. I'll call you later and find out what they told you. Rose, I'm sorry that I pushed you last night to come over. I understand now, why you wanted to be here. I don't believe you're safe right now alone is all."

"I'm sure I will be fine, and Liam, no worries." I reached out to take his cup, and as he passed it to me he let his fingers linger a little too long on mine. My breath sped up, even though I tried to ignore it. Clearing my throat, I turned walking back into the house before my body betrayed me. After placing the dishes in the dishwasher, Liam left following behind me until I turned into the veterinarian's office.

# Chapter Four

Ambling into the veterinarian's office, which always smelled of disinfectant, I waited in the navy vinyl chairs, patiently, for the Doctor to see me. Consulting with Dr. Connolly, privately,

I explained how Pete died. I even offered to send that portion of the video to him along with the police report, but he declined. He sympathized, as I knew he would, stating he knows me and I would never harm Pete. He also gave me a long hug, while he rubbed my back and asked me to dinner tonight, as always, I declined.

After filling out the cremation authorization and paying, I went out to my SUV. Not bearing to watch the doctor, as he personally took Pete's stiffened body out, I had to turn my back and cover my sobs with my hand. I didn't want to remember my poor baby that way.

After starting my SUV, my cell rang. "Hi Bella," I answered after I connected the call, using my button on my steering wheel.

"Ms. Kelly, did you hear from Grace? She went to the pub last night, with the group from work on her motorbike.

The motorbike is here now, but she's not, and she's not answering her cell."

"I haven't heard from her, but I will ring her. I'm sure her phone died. You know how she is. I bet she met a pretty blonde girl, and they've been talking for hours strolling by the canal, drinking wine. She's such a romantic when she first meets someone. I'm sure she's fine. Send me a text if she rings you, alright?"

"Okay, thanks, Ms. Kelly." She said and ended the call. *Shit.*

First, I sent a text to Gracie, then rang her leaving a message on her voicemail. Driving below the speed limit, immersed in thought to Police Service in Belfast fifty minutes away, took well over an hour. Unfortunately, they had no information on my case. The Constables I worked with last night, had gone home already.

Walking out of the Police Service my phone rang with Unknown Number displayed. The caller was most likely a telemarketer. Considering my recent pickle, I immediately stopped walking and answered "Hello?" A weird robotic voice came on, "Leave *The Woman Behind the Glass* beside the green bin, behind the Van Gough Museum in Amsterdam, at midnight Sunday evening or Grace dies. Contact PSNI or Korps Nationale Politie and Grace dies. Come alone or Grace Dies," the call ended.

Cold sweat clung to every body part I had and I saw spots dancing in my vision. I couldn't catch a breath. Complete fear overcame me and I bent over and placed my palms on my knees. The loud thumping heartbeat in my ears was deafening, but I gained small breaths and made my way through. When I didn't think I would pass out anymore, I ran to my SUV, locking myself inside, the first thing I thought of was to call Liam. Shaking so much, I could barely look up his number. "Liam," I begged hysterically. "Liam, they took my

Gracie! They want my Grandfather's painting, or they'll kill my Gracie," I pleaded as I cried. Liam calmly said,

"Darling, breathe. Stop and breathe slowly. In and out. Tell me everything they said word for word." I was frozen solid in shock, I slowed my breathing until I felt like I could speak again.

"They said leave *The Woman Behind the Glass* beside the green bin behind the Van Gough Museum at midnight Sunday night, or they'll kill Grace. If I call the Amsterdam Police or PSNI they will kill my daughter. Her roommate called earlier saying Grace hadn't made it home, but her bike did." Liam asked,

"Where are you now?"

"Police Service, Musgrave. I can't go back in and tell them, they said they'd kill my daughter," I exclaimed through my sobs.

"Drive to Kerberos, I'll meet you there," he said.

"I don't have my access pass from class. My gym bag is at home. What do I do?"

"Drive around back, there will be a garage door with two small metal doors above on either side. Wait there. Stay in your motor. They'll open the garage for you. I only left home, I'll be right behind you. Promise me you won't go anywhere else, Rose."

"I promise. I promise. Okay." I said and ended the call.

#

The robotic voice repeated in my head over and over like a broken record, while I drove to Kerberos. At least my ears stopped ringing like cymbals. That was a plus. Driving around the back for the first time, I stopped in front of the oversized industrial garage door preceded by several three-foot-tall metal bollard posts in front. Two small doors flipped open above either side of the garage door. As I looked up and saw a 50 caliber machine gun inside each one. I'd never seen one in person, before. *OH-MY-GOD!*

My mouth was still dangling wide open in shock as the large garage door began lifting and startled me. I watched as the door lifted and the bollard posts slowly lowered into the concrete below. On the right side, a man dressed like Liam waved me in, with an assault rifle over his shoulder.

*What the ever-loving-fuck, Liam?*

Closing my mouth, I drove my SUV up to the man and rolled down the window as he mimicked with his arm.

"Park wherever you like ma'am. Stay in your vehicle, Boss will walk you in when he gets here." He said, followed by a cheeky smile, and shake of his head. He tapped the car roof for me to move ahead. I nodded in return and parked by what I observed to be the only other door at the opposite end of the structure. Surprisingly, there were a lot of cars here on a Saturday. Liam must be a slave driver. After I waited ten minutes, Liam pulled in to the garage like a bat out of hell. As instructed, I remained in my SUV. Liam quickly walked to my SUV and opened my door. Hesitantly I exited with my purse hanging from my shoulder.

Liam still had one hand on the top of my door as he leaned down to look me in the eye and said.

"Do you trust me *now* to keep you safe, Dearheart?"

"Yes," I answered without hesitation and nodded. With this "Compound" only being the garage, if he couldn't do it, nobody could.

"Aye, let's go on up to my team and brainstorm your phone call. Don't worry, we will come up with a plan to bring your daughter back to ye."

Liam closed my door. Placed his hand on the small of my back, with a smile he led me to his layer. I don't know why God brought this man into my life, but I had a feeling I was about to find out.

He led me to the steel door and bent over for a retinal scan. *Retinal scan?* The door opened, with his hand on the small of my back he led me inside the building. Instantly, I noticed his posture change as he stood taller, chin lifted, grimaced, and exuded an aura of command. I had never seen him this way before. I wasn't sure if I should be frightened or turned on. He's still gooey Liam. *Right?*

He led me down a maze of cinder block corridors, and we entered into an elevator. Once situated, he leaned down and kissed me on the top of my head, smiled, and placed his hand on my waist as if this was our natural behavior. After a biometric scan and one more retinal scan, I made up my mind. Liam didn't only design bespoke security systems, and provide bodyguard services, for the rich and famous that traveled to the Emerald Isle.

After the elevator opened he placed his hand on my lower back again and guided me through a maze of frosted glass offices stopping at one. He entered a code that was way too long for anyone without a memory-enhancing microchip to remember. Once the door opened, I realized this was his office and it was *huge*.

His workspace was a bit disorganized with stacks of folders covered his desk, but he had a fabulous view of Downtown Belfast, with the glass dome from Victoria Square. Turning to the right and spied the biggest television I had ever seen, mounted on the wall, behind a conference table that easily seated twenty. I couldn't stay quiet any longer.

"Holy F-U-C-K Handsome! You aren't restricted to only security systems and bodyguards are you?" I loud whispered in shock and awe. His demeanor had already changed as, his hands were in his pockets, with that sheepish grin that showed his dimples, and he looked up at me and said,

"No. This part of my company isn't for public awareness, Rose. What happens here has to stay here, okay?" Of course, I nodded. I'm good with secrets.

There was a knock at the door and five bearded men nearly the size of Liam walked in and said,

"The Beards have officially joined the party, Boss," as they all sat down around the ginormous table. Next, a stunning 20 something woman, with long blonde hair walked in. She had a tight black pencil skirt, red bottom stilettos on and carried a laptop. She sat down, smiled, and chatted with the Beards. Red hot jealousy ran through my veins.

This supermodel, probably his assistant, works for Liam, and I was worried about when he called me Dearheart, and I slept in his guest room? The Erebus Teams from this morning, Callum, Ian, Matt, and Declan walked in closing the door behind them, and nodded to me as they entered.

Noticing Liam's bad-ass demeanor was back, as he pulled out the chair to the right of the table closest to his, and motioned with his hand for me to sit down. After taking the offered seat, he sat next to me at the head of the table, and with the confidence of a Four Star General, owned the room. He introduced everyone. Sheelagh, who was not his assistant, but his head of Security, sat to his immediate left. *I bet she practiced throat stretches nightly just for this job, in no way could she be that smart.* Lastly, the Beards introduced themselves as not Team Beard, but Team Bravo, Riley, Kian, Kenneth, Owen and Evan.

I repeated the call from the vet's office and explained, "*The Woman Behind the Glass* is a painting my Grandfather completed while at art school in Rome right before WWII. My Grandmother gifted the painting to my Dad after my Grandfather passed away around forty years ago. The painting isn't monetarily valuable, and only special because he painted it in his carefree days of finding himself. He never painted again and the canvas isn't even signed. The painting sits rolled up in the safe room at my house, waiting until I have it professionally framed to hang. Really, I don't think anyone else wanted it. What reason could there be for anyone to want that painting? They can take the damn thing for all I care. I want my daughter back. What about my other girls? What if he tries to take Opal and Lilly?"

"Rosie, give Sheelagh their information, and we'll send Erebus Teams Three and Four on protection detail," Liam instructed. Sheelagh cut in at that moment with her Scottish accent.

"Ms. Kelly, could you please tell us your Grandads name, occupation, and which art school he went to in Italy?"

"His name was Theodore Harris. I'm sorry, but I'm not sure what school he went to, only that it was in Rome just before WWII. He met and married my Grandmother, Maeve, in 1943 after he joined the Navy and came to Florida. He was in the Navy for quite a while after the war and traveled all over the world. When he mustered out, he took the relaxing route and became a farmer. I can call my dad and ask if he remembers anything."

"No worries, I'll find it. We don't want anyone else aware that your daughter is missing. Now tell us about your daughter, Grace," she said cool as a cucumber while she typed. She unnerved me and my knee began to bounce. Liam put a hand on my knee and gave it a gentle squeeze. I relaxed right away. Closing my eyes briefly, I took a relaxing breath and continued.

"Grace is getting her Bachelors in Business at the University of Amsterdam. She's introverted, so she keeps to herself mostly. She likes to go to the pub with her friends, and they attend comic book conventions all over Europe together. Gracie's my little comic book nerd." I smiled as I thought of her and continued, "Here's the last picture I have of her. She's blonde there, but she changes colors regularly," I said as I passed my cell around the table for everyone to see.

"She has a small apartment with her roommate across town. She and her roommate work together part-time at The

Cafe on campus. She rides her yellow Vespa everywhere and would never hurt a soul. Grace is truly the sweetest child. I don't understand why anyone would take her. I would happily just have given them the painting, they didn't have to take my timid little twenty-year-old daughter," I said as a stray tear ran down my face. Liam removed his hand from my knee and held my hand on top of the conference table and gave me a reassuring small smile and sad puppy dog eyes. Wiping off my tear, I peered around the table and every eye was on our clasped hands. One would think they'd never seen anyone in command have friends or family. If they ever found out who my girls' Godfathers were in the US Military, they'd pass out. Unfortunately, the US Army can't help me here.

Evan stared at me and asked with his Northern Irish accent, "What's makes this painting so extraordinary, someone would abduct a twenty-year-old girl? It doesn't make sense." Grunts came from around the table. Sheelagh cut in as she looked at Liam,

"Boss, I'll call the pilot and have the jet for 1800 hours and reserve adjoining suites for you both and Bravo if you like. I'll also research where Ms. Kelly's Grandfather went to art school, and why that painting might be worth stealing." Liam instructed each man on his new task and dismissed them. Still holding my hand, he looked down at me and said,

"Dearheart, I'll drive you home to pick up that painting. We'll bring it back here for Sheelagh to scan in case anything of value is underneath. The Erebus Teams will escort us." I peered up at the men as Liam ordered, "Lookout for tails and, use your coms. Wheels up at 1800 hours." Hoots and hollers followed with a few pats on the back for Liam.

"About time, Brother," Riley stated.

"Welcome to the club, Boss," drawled Kian.

"No doubt you'll mind our man in Amsterdam, Rosie. Welcome to the Clan Kerberos," Declan said as he clapped his hand on my shoulder and squeezed.

*I wasn't sure what was happening, but I'll roll with it.*

# Chapter Five

We stood to leave, and Liam tagged my hand and led me back through the labyrinth and downstairs to his Urban Assault Vehicle. His parking spot had the name, "BOSS" painted on the wall in front of it. *Cocky much?*

Liam drove out of the Kerberos garage, and I turned to Liam, "So tell me, what you actually do for a living, Liam." After a long exhale followed by a few calmed breaths, Liam began,

"I used to be in The Royal Army in a Special Forces Team called the SAS, Sea-Air-Service Regiment. I was a

Special Air Service Operator for twenty-one years, mostly in the Middle East. First, as an active Operator, but as I aged out, I was promoted to Officer Commander. After my convoy was hit by an RPG, a Rocket Propelled Grenade, in a friendly fire incident. Faulty trigger and a green private was all it took. I was forced to retire my commission as disabled unfit for duty. I came back with one less appendage."

Understanding how difficult it was to admit you were broken, I put my hand on top of Liam's and gave it a small squeeze to comfort him. I already thought from his slight limp he wore a prosthetic, like my cousin, but to bare yourself to anyone would be difficult. I should know. Liam immediately turned his hand over, threaded his fingers with mine on the middle console, and continued,

"I started Kerberos in Belfast because there were few Security Services with my background available here. I lived in England for over fifteen years and needed a change.

Glasgow is too busy for me. I prefer the smaller cities and my mam's family is still here. The rest of my family is just a ferry ride away. Sometimes, I fly back on the weekends to catch my nephews' football games.

"I started with the Home Security Division, added the Bodyguard Services, and Sharp Shooter Training, and so on. We train many policing forces throughout Europe and Britain.

"I received a lot of calls requesting some off-books operations overseas. I did it myself for a while, then it became too much on my body. There was a lot of money to be made and I added the Black Operations Division, on a case-by-case basis, for our Allied governments who need deniability, or maintain the impression of neutrality. I added the private sector for High-Value Targets and Hostage Rescue.

I have killed people, darling. A lot of people. I only pulled the trigger when I had to. There were a lot more, I didn't kill because I didn't feel I *had* to pull the trigger. Those I remember more. They usually come back to bite me in the arse. I tell you this in strict confidence. The only people who need to know what we do, find us. We're not exactly a household name and I'd like to keep it that way."

It was a lot to absorb. We pulled up in my driveway without speaking another word. *That's why his demeanor changed.*

Liam told me to stay put as he cleared the house. He waved me in when he was finished. Once in my kitchen, I stood looking down at Pete's food bowl.

*My poor pooch, I'm so sorry. I didn't mean to leave you out there, but it was not safe to reopen the door. I never thought anyone would hurt you, my sweet puppy. You didn't deserve that. I'm so sorry. You'll always be with me. Please forgive me, puppy love.*

We made our way back to my bedroom and I opened the safe room with Liam in tow. Once we were inside, Liam appeared enwrapped in contemplation. Stepping toward him, I inquired, "Are you okay, Liam?" He peered down at me and asked,

"Dearheart, are you alright with everything I told ye knowing I killed in the line of duty?" After a brief moment of searching his sad puppy dog eyes, I finally spoke.

"You have killed people in the military, yes, I'm OK with that. You also protect people and save hostages, which I'm OK with too. You put yourself on the line so the rest of us can be free to do what we want, marry who we want, and believe what we want. Yes, you've killed people, but you're not a killer, Liam. You are our protector. Thank you. Thank you for keeping the rest of us safe so that we can be free."

I lifted my right hand and pointed at him to further my point saying, "*You're* the one who put their lives on the line. *You're* the one who did all the work. It doesn't matter what I think, Liam. It shouldn't matter to you what anyone thinks."

"It matters to me," he warily stated.

At that point, I threw my arms around his middle and pulled him in for a hug. If that was the only way I could convince him, I was good with his job, so be it. Everyone needs to be hugged sometimes, and I could really use one myself. After a few minutes, I reluctantly let him go. Hoping that had made him feel better, I gave him a quick nod before I bent over, avoiding the intimacy and how good he smelled, and intense his tight embrace felt as he rubbed my back nestling his nose in my hair. I now know how hard his abs and pecs are and wonder if his ass is that tight.

I shook it out of my head, picked up the drawing tube. Unscrewing the end, I opened it verifying the painting was still rolled up inside. After tightening the end cap, I turned to the safe. After entering the simple code, I took out my passport and 500 euros in cash. After making sure the safe was locked again, I stood and walked out of the room past Liam, accidentally brushing against his arm. That man lit fires that I never knew existed.

Keeping myself occupied before I embarrassed myself blushing, I grabbed my gym bag. Dumping it out on the bed, I began packing for a few days in Amsterdam. Making sure to pack extra hearing aid batteries, my case, tablet, and chargers. Maybe some dirty laundry would shift him away into the other room. After realizing, my small gym bag wasn't big enough I quickly exchanged my items to my carry on, from under the bed.

#

As we walked to Liam's Rover, my skin crawled and the hair on the back of my neck stood up. I've had this feeling too many times. Making sure to keep my head down, Liam opened my door and I got into the passenger seat making sure to buckle in. Turning to Liam I whispered, "Feels like someone's watching us."

"Is the hair on the back of your neck standing up?" Liam asked.

"Yeah."

"Aye, I sensed it too. A black Mercedes is suspiciously parked down the road behind us." Liam hit his com and relayed, "We have eyes on us,"

Liam got in and backed out of my driveway headed toward Nutt's Corner. The sooner we got to the Motorway the better. I looked over at him, as he spoke, "Don't look, Rose, but you need to bend over and brace yourself with your arms around your calves. Tuck your head in-between for the airbag to deploy over your back. We have a tail to shake and I don't want you harmed if they fire at us."

I bent right over and did as he had asked without argument. This definitely was not comfortable in my tight jeans, but we would arrive alive, or at least I would. I worried about Liam's safety, but I had confidence, he would get us through this cat and mouse chase.

Liam sped down the rural mountainside, Ian and Matt were supposedly in the lead vehicle with Callum and Declan in the rear. Liam clicked his com and instructed, "Scoot to the motorway and try to shake this tango out into the open." We merged on the A52 headed toward the Motorway at a fast clip,

Liam advised he paired his com to the Bluetooth in the Rover. When everything was paired, I could hear everything in live-action, even though I couldn't see it. Liam hit his com again, "Catch that black Mercedes?" Four clicks relayed then Ian chimed in,

"Boss, let me box you in the Green slow lane and position yourself between this lorry in the middle White lane. When the Merc comes up behind the lorry, Dec, hold a steady wall behind me, while Boss takes the exit. The Merc won't be able to exit the motorway for another mile, by then you'll be halfway to Base, Boss."

"Copy that, Ian, both Teams follow our tail and detain the driver for questioning at Tartarus. Don't shoot anyone and for the love of Christ, don't use the PIT Maneuver this time. I'm not buying two new Rovers in one month, over." Declan added,

"Put the pedal down Boss and scoot!"

Four clicks followed as Liam executed the maneuver off the M1 Motorway. Like clockwork, I knew the two Teams followed the Merc, when Declan chimed in, "You're good to go, Boss."

"Ye can sit up now, hen, they're gone. Are ye alright," he checked.

"Yes, just my tummy. I should be fine now that I'm sitting up."

He looked over at me, turned on the air conditioning on full blast making sure all the vents were turned to me and drove toward Base. Liam swerved lanes a few more times, and took another junction exit. I was not sure I could keep the contents of my stomach down.

"Hold tight, Darling," he said. I watched in my side mirror as the second Merc followed his swift change from the Green to Red lanes, then back again. Liam turned to back to me and instructed,

"Rose, bend over again. I'm sorry, but we have another tail."

"Do what you have to do." I squeaked out as I bent over. He raced down the M3, again. Just before the M3 ended he yelled, "Hold on, Honey!" He hit the brakes and completed a narrow U-turn into the oncoming lane. The tires on his Urban Assault Vehicle screamed in protest as I covered my head preparing, for his Rover to roll over. The Merc missed the turn and barreled down the highway. "I don't think you're supposed to make a U-turn on the highway, Liam. He laughed and responded, "Och! There's no sign! You can pop up now."

We sped our way back through the Titanic Quarter to Base, Liam tapped his cell, hit a speed dial commanding, "Coming in hot, three minutes!" I looked behind us but saw no sign of the Mercedes. Liam instructed, "Darling, stay there till we're in the garage, aye?" A nod and a smile was his answer as I caught a glimpse of him grinning at me, from behind the wheel. He was spectacularly fetching in his element. This would be fun if lives weren't at stake. It's like driving home from school with my Grandpa again.

As he rounded the last corner, I turned to see the turrets were open, with two manned 50 caliber machine guns facing the back entrance. Liam wasn't slowing down and alarm set in. My eyes got huge and my breathing sped up as I raised my arms over my face for impact and screeched. The security bollards quickly dropped seconds before he flew into the back garage. Once inside, I turned to see the bollards immediately lift, and the steel security door dropped. Liam slammed on his breaks nearly to a stop, grinning and laughing.

Turning into his parking spot again, I prayed I wouldn't throw up in his Rover. I grabbed hold of the door handle, swiftly unbuckled myself, and jumped out of the SUV. Bent over, with my hands on my knees trying to get enough air in my lungs. I saw Liam texting someone, then he turned to me laughed and asked,

"You alright? You should have seen your face," he said as he smiled.

"Of course, are you?"

"Aye." He stated, still smiling and nodded. And just like that, my crimson was returned along with a big smile.

"That was insane, Liam. You should add stock car driver to your CV. I should take you to the Brickyard. You know, my brother-in-law designs race cars. I bet he'd soup up your ride." I said smiling.

"Aye, haven't done that in a few weeks," He said as he chuckled with a smile.

*Not sure what I should say to that.*

# Chapter Six

Snatching drawing tube and my purse we walked to the entrance of Liam's Universe. He sent a quick text to someone and scanned his eyeballs again. Gently, he placed his hand on the small of my back and led me to the elevator. Cool calm and collected he seemed as I was still trembling from the adventure. Why do I feel so safe in his presence? I feel as if I could play hide-and-seek with him in this maze of hallways, without a care in the world. How does he do that to me?

Once we were situated in the elevator, Liam smiled, tagged me around my shoulders and kissed the side of my head. Wrapping my arm around his waist was a last reassurance that I was alright. Shaking my head, I gave him a smile and small chuckle in return, and went up to Sheelagh's office.

Taking the tube, Sheelagh carefully removed the painting from the drawing tube, unrolling the canvas for scanning. Liam snagged an unopened cold can of cola off her desk, popped the tab, and handed it to me. I don't think anyone opened my pop for me since I was a kid. Nodding in thanks, I promptly took small sips of the icy-cold drink, to calm my tumbled stomach. Once Sheelagh scanned my painting about sixteen different ways, and left the canvas on the table-sized scanner, she walked to her desktop to retrieve the images.

"This will take a little while to see what the different ultraviolet light scans retrieved. Are you going to your office, Boss," she inquired, looking up at Liam.

"No, we're packing what we need from the Armory, then we'll grab something in the kitchen," Liam explained.

"Sounds good, I'll advise when I'm ready to present my findings." Sheelagh stood turned to me, and held out a cell phone to me and declared, "Ms. Kelly, here is your new satellite mobile, it's been encrypted and contains tracking software. Pray never needed, we can always find you. I took the liberty of changing your provider, to keep your old number. Your mobile hasn't received any data in the last hour if you had not already realized." With that, I came entirely out of my motion sickness stupor. Straightening my back, I lifted my chin defiantly, and took a deep breath preparing for confrontation. *How dare her.*

Liam has seen what was coming and stepped back. He crossed his arms as he leaned against the far wall. I'm not sure if he hoped to stay out of my line of fire, or if he was in this with her. Probably the latter. I turned to Sheelagh, who still held out the phone to me, and began in my best-sugared bitch voice,

"Thank you for your thoughtfulness, however, I don't require a new phone. Mine works just fine and I would rather not receive the bill from a satellite phone. We're on a grandfathered family contract, and I don't plan on changing. Please switch the number back."

Refusing to take the phone from her, I took one step back. She turned to Liam and silently asked for help. Liam's lips were in a straight line and his nose flared. Obviously he disliked my response. He was surely in this with her. Taking the phone from Sheelagh, he snatched my left-hand, and placed the phone in my grasp. I tried to hand the phone back to him, but he refused. Gently, I placed the phone on Sheelagh's desk. "Liam," I started, but he interrupted me with his furrowed brow, and placed his hands on his hips, giving himself a severe appearance.

"Rose, this is for your protection and my peace of mind. If you're taken, my team may not be able to get you to safety unharmed. Your house was destroyed, dog killed, daughter kidnapped, and not one but two motors chasing us. Think of your girls. They would want their mam safe. Please, Darling, for them and for me," he looked down at me begging with those puppy dog eyes. That gave me pause. Liam was right. Looking up at him I gave in with shame and silent fury. I'm not one of his minions, but knowing better, I won't put him in his place in front of one of them.

I nodded but had to say my piece. I pointed at him and stated, "I understand this is important for now even though I keep *you* close, but when this is all over, I'm giving this back to you." Liam took two steps forward gently taking my upper left arm in his right hand, and leaned his head down to my ear. With his hot breath on my neck, he exhaled, and said,

"We'll see, Darling."

I shivered and my cheeks and chest started to heat up. Unable to control my body, my thighs automatically clenched together. He lightly kissed my cheek slowly, letting his lips linger. He leaned back slightly and donned a smug smile. He added a cheeky wink, put his hand on my lower back again, and led me out of Sheelagh's office to the elevator. *Damn my body.*

My stomach had begun to feel much better the more we walked. I can't see how I thought this labyrinth of an old warehouse was strictly bodyguards, gymnasiums, and alarms. I kept waiting for the Goblin King in a bad wig to appear. After the elevator, two more concrete hallways, and three more retinal scans, we entered the Armory and I met Tom, or should I say... Alfred.

"Holy hand grenades Batman, any more wonders in your Secret Underground Layer? A pool full of sharks, maybe?" I exclaimed with my mouth agape. Both Liam and

Tom's heads fell back in a roar of laughter. I looked around my immediate area and stated, "There're enough guns and knives in here to secure a small country. I'm not sure what those tubes over there are," I said and waved my hand in the direction of a crate on the floor in an opened cage.

Liam strolled over to the wooden crate I had waved at. He picked up a long tube, threw it on top of his shoulder, with a huge smile his eyes lit up like a little boy, and he said,

"This is our newest model Shoulder Mounted Rocket Launcher, but I don't think we'll need that this go."

"Oh, yeah, my dad worked on some sort of component that went inside one of those years ago. Maybe the tomahawk, no, that was before in the submarine. No, it wasn't. It was a surface-to-air missile or something like that. I don't know. He was at Twenty-nine Palms for a good while." Befuddled, Liam turned around, furrowed his brows and said,

"Ye care to explain that, hen?" I broke out in a laugh, shaking my head and explained,

"I really shouldn't. Most of my life, I told people he was an engineer. I mean, I thought he was until I was about thirty-five, but he's not." I said as I shook my head. "He's super smart, and I'm not complaining, since I keep my own Wikipedia at the end of the phone line. He can tell you everything from which kind of glue to use to what happens to tectonic plates during an ice age. You can ask him next time they're here for a visit." Liam smiled and went about putting his shoulder-mounted toy away.

I realized, I may have given him the approval to meet my parents, I tried to back-step and said, "I'm sure you could blow him away with your useful knowledge of being "Captain Bad Ass" and all. Do you have a cape?" Liam clued in and cocked his crooked smile. He added a wink, and a chin lift, and he corrected,

"That's Officer Commander Bad Ass, Dearheart."

*Touche*

I shook my head and walked around, and looked at all the guns and rifles on display. Some of them I had used before, but most of them I had no business touching, like the automatic rifles. They were all properly oiled and I certainly *did not* want my fingerprints on any of them. I walked over to a crate of grenades, trying not to smirk, pointed to the crate and questioned, "If I pull that ring, will the top pop off and a bunch of snakes jump out at me?" Liam and Tom lost themselves running over to make sure I didn't touch any. After I bent over laughing, slapping my knee, they walked away smiling and shaking their heads.

Everything else was behind locked welded wire Armory cages. Complete with signs indicating electric shock if touched, just like my mothers. Liam took an extra-large duffel from the cabinet and started filling the bag while Tom, marked each item and quantity on the list. By the time the guys walked over to the standing desk to sign the paperwork an hour later, I was falling asleep on my feet and completely bored.

Sitting on the chair, I picked up the desk phone and said, "Yes, I'll order The Batmobile, Lasso of Truth, and a slingshot on the side, with ketchup." A roar of laughter erupted and I turned around, realizing it wasn't just the three of us because the Beards had just entered Liam's Toy Store. After Liam and I received quite a few pats on the back, hoots, and hollers, I received several kisses on the cheek and was lifted off the floor for a milkshake hug from some ginger Beard. Liam was visibly pissed.

Liam actually growled, muttered something incoherent, grabbed my hand and led me to the kitchen. I expected a small microwave room for staff, but instead it was a huge military kitchen. Just like my Grandpa said he used to cook in for the Navy. Shiny stainless steel cupboards, tables, and appliances donned every wall with at least a twenty-foot island in the middle for food prep. Liam carried leftover containers from the walk-in refrigerator and placed them on the gleaming counter.

"Spaghetti Bolognese or Cottage Pie?" he offered.

'Cottage Pie, please, I'll grab the plates if you tell me where they are."

"Och, no I got it, I'm an old pro at eating leftovers on off-hours. Keeps me from having to cook at home" he said.

"You cook?"

"How else would I eat?" Liam challenged through his laugh.

"I guess I'm just not used to a man cooking, grilling maybe. My Grandpa used to make sauerkraut boiled with potatoes and hot dogs, or SOS sometimes. That was his specialty. Liam raised his eyebrow and asked,

"What's SOS?"

"Shit on a Shingle."

"Aye, tell me it's a name for something else," he said with his eyebrow cocked.

I laughed, "Chipped Beef and white gravy on toast, with canned peas on the side. You've never had SOS, Officer Commander Bad Ass?"

"No," he replied shaking his head.

"Well, next time the company comes from the States, I'll add dried beef to the toll list."

"Toll list? You make people bring things to you when they visit?"

"Yeah, in exchange for free room and board, I give them a shortlist of items I can't get here or online. I ask for boxed macaroni shells and cheese, canned chili peppers, season salt, old-fashioned root beer, and cold-processed kosher dill pickles; I miss those the most, but sometimes I change it up. Every once in a while, another Ex-Pat will post on social media they found something at a grocery store, but they're always too far away to warrant the trip. I have gotten quite good at making some things homemade, but sometimes you can't create a substitute. Imagine a bunch of Americans, on the sly, huddled over a trunk in the grocery's car park. Hey man, how much for that mac 'n cheese?" We both chuckled at the thought.

After everything Liam had done for me, I found myself wanting to know more about him. What makes him tick? Once our food was reheated, as we sat down at the counter and began to eat, I asked,

What's your story, Liam?"

He lifted one eyebrow and asked, "What do you mean, what's my story?"

"Everybody has a story like what you majored in college, have you ever been married, or do you have kids." I ran through the scenarios. Liam nodded his head and pinched his brows together in contemplation.

"Aye, I was married for about five years. We met after secondary school in College and married right after. Shortly after that I joined the British Army and was sent to the Gulf War. While deployed, I realized I wanted to do more. I could do more. I applied for Selection with the SAS. Helen agreed, at first, but later said I was never home enough to warrant having children. I was gone most the time, and we weren't really happy. She never wanted to talk about anything important, and I think she kind of preferred things that way. We were young, only twenty when we married and matured differently. I matured in war, and she went a whole other way.

"I was scheduled to go for Close Quarter Battle exercises in Perth, and she told me that if I left, she wouldn't be there when I got back." After a long pause, Liam looked over at me and spoke again. "The SAS teaches you to be honest with yourself. Know what your strengths and weaknesses are, and know what you want and why you want it.

"I didna want to be married anymore and neither did she. We were strangers living in the same flat who never talked, but had a piece of paper that said we were married. I loved her, but I was no longer in love with her, and she felt the same way. I had orders that I couldna change and said we would talk about it when I got back. When I returned a few months later, her things were gone and there was a letter from her solicitor in the mail slot stating she had filed for divorce."

"I'm so sorry, Liam," I said and I took his hand in mine. Liam rubbed my fingers with his thumb and continued.

"Nothing to be sorry about, Dearheart. You cannot help who you love and who you don't. Love doesn't keep a timetable. You can fall in love without noticing and last for a lifetime, or be gone in a flash if you don't nurture the relationship. If I had stayed, possibly, we could have worked through it somehow, but I won't live in the past. I made my choices and we're done. Besides, she's much happier now, married to a few kids, from what I hear."

Once we finished eating, Liam and I loaded the industrial dishwasher and cleaned up our mess. He led me back through his Labyrinth back up to his office. After a quick text, Sheelagh and the Beards reappeared and our next meeting began, without Riley.

"Today it pays to be a winner, lads, the scan showed nothing beneath the painting, however, I did find a hidden signature in the painting itself. I called my contact at the Louvre, and the painting was not by Ms. Kelly's Granddad, but by one Johannes Helmsmeier." Whistles rang out around the table as Sheelagh continued,

"Ms. Kelly, I'm sorry but your Granada was never enrolled in an art class in Italy, He was an operative for the OSS. That's the Office of Strategic Services."

"Yes, I'm aware of what it is," I grumbled. Trying to shut her up.

"His mission was to be Johannes's protection detail while he was enrolled there in Art School, then hand him off to the Navy. We believe Helmsmeier gave him the painting then, because my contact also found a hidden date in the hair. There were other hidden markings, like coordinates and references to other pieces that I am still working on. Regardless, it is believed to be his last painting because Helmsmeier was found dead one week after the Navy sent him into hiding in The Orkney's in Scotland.

"Shortly after WWII began, your Granddad was recruited to what was known as The Amphibious Scout and Raider School in Florida. He was on one of the original UDT (Underwater Demolition Teams) members, and one of the first frogmen. They are now called Navy SEAL's."

Completely angered that a Scot dare recite my country's history, I rudely interrupted,

"Yeah, my cousin is a SEAL. Pensacola is where my Grandparents met. They lived in Florida when my

Grandmother was a secretary for the Navy. He told me he was a cook on a ship. Why didn't I see this coming? I have all his Navy things, his pea coat, bed-roll, mess kit. You'd think he would leave a secret message in the pocket saying, "Sorry, Sugar, but I was really a bad-ass super spy specializing in explosive ordinances."

"Ms. Kelly. He wouldn't have been able to tell anyone and I doubt even your Granny would have been aware. They were very secretive back then."

"Yeah, I'm familiar. Most of my family has a military background. What I don't understand is why he was so proud to take us to the Navy Yard in Pensacola and not Fort Pierce. That must have been where my Grandmother worked. He even took us to eat at his old mess hall. He wouldn't have access to the Army base after. I think they secretly trained the first UDT men there," I muttered to myself.

Riley walked in and took his seat at the table.

"How did the interrogation go?" Liam inquired.

"Turns out, Helmsmeier put a price of £2M to whomever brings the painting in first." Whistles came from around the table. The Intel gets better, Wilhelm Helmsmeier is the one who has set the price. Turns out he's Johannes's Grandson's been collecting the paintings, through questionable means, for the last twenty years stating they belong to him. This is the last one, which is why he's so eager to possess the painting by any means. As we're already aware, he's been working with the Italian Mafia for a while, and is wrapped in a current deal with them on an old Greek statue."

"Belfast International, wheels up in two hours," Liam quizzed Sheelagh.

"Yes, Boss. I reserved the top floor of The Grand European Amsterdam Hotel. This hotel is nearest the Van Gough Museum with available suites. Access to the floor will be restricted to Kerberos and wait staff only. And, if I may, Boss, would you be able to take two ticks to go over another investigation with me?"

"Email me and I'll review the file on the plane," Liam responded.

Once everyone else left the office, I quickly left Kylie a voicemail asking her to manage the cafe as I had to go see Grace on short notice. Hopefully, she won't ask more. Kylie was our closest friend from the Shelter and I never keep things from her. If not for Liam, she would be my first call. Being another American from abroad, we were instantly bound. She's close to all of us and our biggest ally from abroad. I'm so thankful she and her daughter have been gifted into our lives.

Liam picked up his pack and bag of toys, and looked up, and smiled. His dimples showed, and I was pretty sure he knew. They were his secret weapons of seduction. You didn't realize they were there until he brought them out and used them against you. Every time he did, I couldn't help but smile. He was contagious, even in these dire circumstances.

I wonder what he looks like under that trimmed beard. I bet he would look positively dreamy with dark scruff. Man, I would want to lick his dimples then. How far his scar does goes down his face, I wonder. His beard covers most of it. I wonder if he'd ever shave his facial hair for me. Would he let me see the whole Liam?

He tipped his head to the door as we needed to leave. "Should I text Opal and Lilly now, or wait until we're in Amsterdam," I questioned.

"Text them now Darling," he suggested.

I quickly sent two texts, and hoped to avoid an inquisition on our recent predicament. I gathered my purse and the drawing tube and walked to the elevator with Liam. Only then, I saw he had a secretary's desk I hadn't noticed before. I wonder what his secretary was like. He certainly put himself on the line financially, with this enormous black operations venture. After seeing him in action, I had enough confidence in him to say he seems exceptionally knowledgeable about his job. He commands with such intimidation, thankfully, I'm not one of his troopers.

As he walked in front of me through the maze and opened doors for me, I couldn't help but to look at his ass. He has the best ass. I wonder what he would look like in 501's and a pair of cowboy boots. Knowing my body, I would probably faint right there beet red and drooling.

We walked to his black Rover and began our drive to Belfast International. I never cared much for this drive, as I always got lost. My Grandpa would say I couldn't find my way out of a paper bag. My knee kept bouncing and Liam placed his hand on my leg to stop me. I needed to break the tension, from the task at hand and turned on the radio without permission. Ciaran would have immediately switch it off. After I scanned a few channels, and not finding anything I liked I turned to Liam and asked, "Do you mind if I pair my phone and put on something from my playlist?"

"Whatever you want, Dearheart," he drawled.

I paired my new phone and logged in to my online music account. Before I thought better of it, I put on my dance playlist I usually play in the kitchen with Pete. Before too long, Liam sang and head-bopped along with me. I lifted my arms and motioned with the lyrics, drum, and guitar solos. Liam had an amazing voice. We couldn't stop laughing. I needed this. Closer to the airport, I confessed.

"Thank you, I needed a stress break. Pete and I danced to this playlist while I cook dinner every night and cleaned. It helped me relax and Pete loved it like playtime. I play a few instruments and I get lost for hours when I do. It opens my soul and I fall in love with the music all over again. Playing slow pieces, he would lay at my feet the whole time and usually fall asleep. I think he liked the vibrations."

"I saw a few in your conservatory. Do you play them all," he asked.

"Not at all, the brass and woodwinds are Gracie's. The guitar and ukulele are Opals. The cello is Lilly's. The piano and violin are mine. Gracie and Opal play a little piano, as well. Sometimes Kylie will bring her saxophone, and we jam to old songs when the girls are home. It's fun." I smiled remembering.

"When did you start playing," he asked.

"I started when I was seven. I came home after my music teacher had several of her sorority sisters come in and play for us and teach us about the different instruments. I wanted to play the violin and my parents rented me one. They paid for private instruction.

"As I got older, I joined the local symphony made up of high school students. We had concerts and played with the local Philharmonic on occasion as well. You get used to playing with a huge audience, but an audience of 2500 was a bit intimidating when you're so young. Someone donated season tickets to the Philharmonic Season every year, so we'd get all dressed up in our Sunday best. I'd ask my friends or family, and they would accompany me. In the nosebleed section of course.

"I was selected to accompany Yo-Yo Ma with the Philharmonic once. That was a treat. The entire Opera House was packed. Our conductor, who was also the conductor of the

Philharmonic, loved my playing. He told my mother I was brilliant. I had some huge flaws, and I never would have called myself that. She didn't tell me that for years. Most likely because I wouldn't have continued to push myself if she had.

"I knew I was better than most and I always won every scholarship I tried out for. It became a given and all the other players would be upset. It paid for music camps at the state university in the summers. Of course, I went and made a lot of friends. We had some good times. I stopped playing after I got married. He said I sucked. About five years ago, I took it up again." Before I knew it, we were at the airport.

# Chapter Seven

Once we began taxiing down the runway on the private plane, out of habit with my past history of airsickness, I reached over and closed all the window shades near me. Liam sat next to me, of course. Hesitantly, he asked,

"Don't you like to view the countryside on liftoff?"

"I don't want to be motion sick again. Once we're above the clouds and stop climbing, my stomach will settle and I'll reopen them for you," I explained. At my response, Liam nodded and put his hand on my bouncing knee as we taxied down the runway. Instantly somewhat calmer, I closed my eyes, tipped my head back, and attempted to relax.

Once the seat belt sign chimed off and my stomach

was settled, I unbuckled and reached to open the window

shades, but Liam stopped me saying,

"Leave them, Sugar. I need to read about the delay in

that project for Sheelagh." That truly rubbed me the wrong

way. Drawing the line and calmly said, "Liam, you're not

allowed to call me Sugar. Only my Grandparents called me

that. Sweet Lovey, Irish Rose, or Sweetheart, my other

Grandfather called me those." Liam smiled at my defiance and

winked as he said,

"I'll stick to Dearheart, then, hen." I couldn't help but

smile and shake my head. I don't dare peer over at him, I knew

he'd flashed those dimples again. *This man!*

Liam removed his laptop from his computer bag and

placed it on the table in front of him, he booted up. Liam put

his reading glasses on and I nearly lost myself. I had to clamp my thighs together. Talk about a *hot* librarian moment. He looked so distinguished in those tortoiseshell frames, I could only imagine what he'd look like in a tailored suit. *Distract yourself with your music, Rose.*

Taking out my phone I started my relaxed playlist and paired with my hearing aid. A few moments later, I peered over at Liam's laptop and spied a photo of an old vault. Pausing my playlist I changed channels on my bionic ear, turning to Liam I asked,

"Do you mind if I take a look at that?"

"I can't share this, hen. I'm under contract," Liam gently declared.

"I'm sure your contract states, you can outsource to third parties. Because of that, you can outsource it to me. I studied my vaults and this one is a goldmine. Tell me about it." I said in a manner of complete confidence.

"Aye, as long as you keep the file to yourself then," he said and turned the laptop, so I could share the screen. "You likely heard on the news, a major heist took place at the First High Street Bank Safe-Deposit Vault on Thursday night. We're advising their security department on possible solutions. No one can figure out how they got in and out without anyone tripping any alarms. Nothing is on the cameras and no prints were found."

"I don't watch much TV, but I worked for and managed different clusters of bank branches throughout my career. I was always fascinated by how people thought they could pull these things off. They come up with the craziest disguises. My predecessor gave me access to an online manager's forum, where we could post what currency was taken and how across the country. Robberies that are under

10K a lot of them don't even hit the news. I'll keep confidentiality. This will be so much fun!"

Liam hesitated looking at me like I was nuts, then nodded, "Alright, show me what you've got."

"This is an outdated vault. My best guess is about a century old or more. This vault only has two combination dials on the front, not three. That's odd in itself. Are there more photos or do you have any of the model numbers, and can you cast them up on that big TV, so we can view the entire image?"

"Kian, switch on that TV above you, please," he asked. Liam took the laptop back and cast his laptop to the large screen after minimizing the photo to fit the screen, I asked,

"Can you please scan through any other photos in the file, please?

"Liam flipped through a few when I said, "Stop."

Liam did, and I proceeded to stand and squeeze past him to the TV when we hit a pocket of turbulence. He grasped my waist as I fell backward and landed on his lap. My body heated and he said through his chuckle,

"If you wanted to sit on my lap, Darling, all you had to do was ask."

Red-faced, I breathed heavy and perspired, I couldn't turn around and be enamored with his seductive dimples, glasses and smile. The turbulence ended and I stood, so he had to release me, and walked to the mounted TV. *God, his hands on me felt so good.*

I scanned to where the old vaults cornered each other turned to Liam and asked, "Are there any more photos of the vault's ceiling? Also, I'll need the schematics of that model vault door." When I turned around, I realized I had everyone's attention.

"Ceiling?" Liam asked with one eyebrow perched up.

"Yeah, the ceiling," Confirming by nodding my head.

After a moment of scanning through his photos, Liam, cast several more photos of the top of the vault, and a false ceiling. "Are the basement blueprints in the file?" After Liam cast the image, I pointed to the toilets, which were right next to the vault as usual, I pondered allowed, "Do you have a map of the tunnels they used two hundred and fifty years ago, and photos of the ceiling and walls in the toilets, including behind the wall mirror?"

"Aye, I'll inquire if there are some, why?" Liam questioned with his brows scrunched together.

"Go back to the original photo of the vault, please." Pointing to the photograph of the vaults I continued, "This vault screams major security problems. The vault is very old, therefore, this is only a room in the basement with a steel front and vault door. The walls are most likely not reinforced with concrete. Today banks use an entire steel-reinforced, nearly impenetrable, independent structure. The safe deposit boxes are now built into the concrete walls. The safe-deposit boxes that are here are independent. They're free-standing structures made of brushed stainless steel which is too heavy to move unless the bank itself relocates."

I pointed to the top of the structures, as I continued. "Looking to where these two corners of the independent structures meet along with the corner of the vaults on the next wall, remains an empty square where someone small, about the size of a teenager, could slip into.

"This bank was so old, the tunnels may lead right to the back; as the bank was built next to the courthouse in those days for security. The courthouse also contained the jail in the basement, back then. The tunnels connected all the buildings in the row and this vault is at the back wall of the bank's basement. Jail cells are under the courthouse as well. They used to use the tunnels to march the Irish prisoners out to be hung due to their beliefs. I'm sure you understand how wrong that was." Everyone responded with a nod in agreement. *Good.*

"Regardless, from using this bank lobby myself, the upstairs was updated so that all the tellers, or tills, are behind bullet-resistant glass now, making an old-fashioned hold-up unheard-of these days. Most bank robberies are done with a pen anymore, or I guess now, maybe the keyboard. The basement, however, is not updated. I'm seeing only one old analog camera and no motion detectors, or noise sensors on the walls. These images don't show any air vent or wall phone either. The vault boxes are too old for heat sensors or pressure plates, unless they were added later. I don't see any wires, did they add them later?" Liam looked intrigued and shook his head.

"Good, Banks don't upgrade their security until they are either robbed, bought out, or remodeled. Their security department is generally run by senior personnel where they spent their entire career in the same bank. They can't see the forest for the trees. There are a few plausible scenarios.

"Number one is always, this was an inside job. Especially, with only two combination locks on the vault and not three. Also, the possibility arises that one of the primary staff, had one combination already; taking the other combination envelope out of the lockbox, and opened the vault themselves. The thief could've even watched the other person dial their combination. The same personnel do it every day, however, the procedure is to turn your head away for privacy. I would find out when the combinations were changed last. It's a possibility, the thief took the envelope that contained the combination before it ever made it into the lockbox outside the vault. But they would have been on the hall camera. It's even possible, they haven't had the combination changed in twenty years and both combinations are the same, and I've seen that too. Is the hallway camera digital or analog?"

Liam answered, "Digital."

"That might rule that out, then. Another plausible scenario is, the robber gained access to the vault via the bathrooms false ceiling and hid in the empty square until the vault was closed that night. Usually, the bathrooms are checked during closing procedures, but if the thief was already in the false ceiling, no one would be the wiser. Once they lifted themselves out of the square after the vault closed; the one analog camera line was cut, right next to the square, and drilled the locks with a cordless drill. Because that's all it takes, just like drilling the locks on an older car to steal its contents.

"Once the thief removed what they wanted from their selected boxes; presumably the largest ones on the far wall separated from the other vault boxes, with a different numbering system. The robber would return to the square. Banks don't leave bags of money laying out like in the movies. The only bags there are full of coin, *if* they own a coin counter machine, which is rare nowadays. They would be too heavy for most to lift and frankly not worth the time unless they're pounds.

"Whether they went through the false ceiling to the bathroom I'm not sure. I would ask if they had a toilet out of service the next day. Possibly, the robber just sat in the bathroom until the bank opened and walked right out. Bathrooms never contain cameras by law, and no one pays attention to who walks in *and* out. Also, check behind that wall mirror. It could have been removed, and the tunnel access point could be right there.

"Another scenario is, the robber went through the tunnels, dismantled the three-hundred-year-old stone wall, and then cut a hole in the wall behind the square to gain access. Cut the camera feed, drilled the boxes, emptied them, and left-back through the square hole to the tunnels. They would need to reseal the wall or a draft or rats would come in, which would give them away. Which boxes were open?"

"The odd-numbered large vaults that were separated," Liam confessed studying his laptop.

"Surprisingly, we have no close-ups of them. Were they drilled?"

"Aye," Liam agreed nodding his head.

"Do you have a close-up of the vault camera and would you cast it please, zooming in on the cuts?"

"Aye," Liam cast the photo.

"The cord was cut from above that vault corner for sure, and at a downward angle. There are even hesitation marks where they attempted the first cut." Liam nodded in agreement. "Please, go back to the last photo." Liam did as I asked.

I nodded as well, as I continued to study the photo on the TV, I noticed something I missed before. "These vault faces appear spotless and shiny, Liam. You might want to check out how long ago the bank had the safety deposit vault doors professionally cleaned. They aren't done very often, only every five years or so at best. The tops of the vaults are spotless, which is abnormal. Especially, if they went through the false ceiling, it would always have dust bunnies at least, as the vault floor is only vacuumed and top-shelf cleaning is never ordered, as it would inconvenience the staff. The cleaner also would recognize which vaults had the most activity with dirty hands. A teller's hands are always filthy with ink from counting the currency. I used to joke the bank was the only place I had to wash my hands before *and* after I used the bathroom.

"Anyone that had experience with what they were looking at, would be clued into the missing security measures. I mean, they stopped allowing false ceilings in vaults over forty years ago in the States. They also had to install air vents and phones for accidental lock-ins or robberies gone wrong. That happened to a friend of mine." Liam interrupted and asked,

"Your friend was accidentally locked inside the vault," he inquired smiling.

"Unfortunately, no, she was locked in naked, with her naked coworkers, in a robbery gone wrong. It was purely for the psychological effect. Anyone would be more interested in covering themselves from their coworkers than charging the robbers, or running out of the building. I affirmed." Liam's smile faltered, and he shook his head in disbelief. Fortunately, he only knew part of the whole terrible story. I continued,

"Only someone that works or used to work at a bank would possess the knowledge of which ones are the Vault Tellers, unless they are the specialized steel cleaner. They would be recognized as the ones with the most hand prints and key scratches around the keyholes. Those are always the larger vaults boxes because the kilos take up so much room." I said as I shook my head.

"Kilo's," Liam said with a smirk on his face. I smiled in return and continued and gestured with my palms.

"We used to call the large blocks of currency kilos, as they're the size of two housing bricks, wrapped in plastic when they are delivered by armored services. They look like kilos of cocaine from the movies. We had to unwrap them, count them, strap them, and band them for auditing." I said with a chuckle. Now that I think about it, it is a funny analogy.

"Thursday night and Monday night have always been the key times for a vault heist or bank robbery. Their cash would be delivered by an armored vehicle late Thursday for payday on Friday. Monday, all the cash from the local High Street business would be deposited. The vault wouldn't sell as much on Tuesday as they would have bought for Thursday. The armored truck wouldn't pick it up Monday's excess until Tuesday morning.

"This week, Friday was the first, meaning the most cash-bought from armored services would have been the peak for that month. Also, this vault is carpeted, as are most. Ask who vacuums their vault and if their background checks and prints are on file. Lastly, find out about the security checks on the vault cleaning specialists. Is it the employees or cleaning staff that's guilty? What are your thoughts? Did I give you any insight?" I looked over at Liam as I finished.

All eyes were locked on me and everyone was quiet as church mice. Liam spoke first. "Aye, I'll email Sheelagh and advise her on it," Liam affirmed with a face full of contemplation. I walked back to my seat after I received several hoots and hollers from the Beards. Liam tagged my hips with his hands as I scooted past him this time. He was probably waiting to catch me again. Turning to me, he surprised me with his commendation saying,

"That was amazing, Dearheart. I had no idea you worked in a bank. I just assumed you always worked in a restaurant or stayed home with the girls. Truly, I'm impressed. Have you done much public speaking, because you nailed it?"

"You sound surprised. Stay at home moms aren't zombies in yoga pants you know. We all have our careers, degrees, and brains intact. People easily forget that while we're working at home raising the next generation of voters. I did a lot of public speaking when I had to command my staff. I occasionally speak for a few local charities and the media as well. You become desensitized to it," I said with a smile.

"I used to be a professional with an actual career, working for *the man* in the real world. My dad suggested it and I started when I was nineteen. After I got my bachelor in Business Management, as soon as I felt comfortable, I got promoted up the ladder again. I learned everything I could along the way. One of the better banks I worked for, gave forgery classes, where we learned how to re-emboss credit cards, or demagnetize and wash checks. They taught us counterfeit construction and the anti-counterfeiting measures the mint makes. Money laundering and counterfeiting was a big one about the time I left. You need to know what to look for and why.

"I ran all the branches in the state of one bank I worked for. They brought me in specifically to find an embezzling employee, and yes, I found her. Unfortunately, I needed regular communication with the Secret Service, the SEC and FBI, and had testified in court for the bank over what some of my customers did. Bankruptcy court, stolen RV's used for meth labs, and parted out Motorcycles. You have adults come in smiling after their parents passed away, greedy for their life savings. Bio-hazard money even came up once, after the "evidence" was released. That was a disgusting one.

"You enter foreclosed properties after murders and other crimes have taken place, and the customers were either dead or in jail. Walking around, I saw bloody mattresses in the loft in the barn, and trunks of children's clothes at a pedophiles house. I nearly lost my composure that day with the Sheriff.

The deputies didn't believe it was necessary in their investigation to take the items, or so they told me. I had to arrange locksmiths, cleaning crews, appraisers, and a Realtor.

"Inspecting that property, I noticed the beautiful home next door was vacant. I walked around and found older marked graves with animal collars. Makeshift crosses aligned them printed with cat and dog names. The Sheriff's Department didn't realize, the man's dead in-laws owned the foreclosed property next door. It was a small community and the gossip was rampant. I was nosey and took a look around. They had to come out and drag Ground Penetrating Radar over the area and found six more bodies. They only did that after I insisted on it. The Deputies were comfortable assuming they were animal graves. You should never *assume* anything with a criminal. I still pray for those children. Everyone has a bank account and or mortgage. Even the criminals. I'm sure your career was the same."

Liam hadn't moved in shock with his mouth agape. Quickly changing the subject, I proceeded, "I'd actually never worked in a restaurant before I opened the café, and Business Management isn't that hard on a small scale. We make coffee, send their burger orders to the kitchen, and pay the bills. The cafe is low stress for me and easy. No more going into a creepy pedophile's kill farm alone, that's for sure. The stories I could tell. I do miss the excitement of the first walkthrough, though. I'm sure you could tell stories, if you weren't bound by secrecy."

"I worked primarily in Counter-Terrorism, with some Human Trafficking. Do you want to open up more cafes' in the future," deflecting again, he asked.

"No," I said and shook my head. "I like the small setup. Anything more and it would run my life. I don't want anything or anyone dictating my life but me. I'm not sure I want to have the cafe permanently, even. It is fine for now. It pays the bills and gives me something to do. If something happens to me, it will provide a steady income for my girls."

Liam was way more than I expected him to be. He listens to what I say without judgment. Unlike Ciaran, he never called me stupid, or said I had no idea what I was talking about. He'd gone out of his way, like no other to protect me, and he listens. He treats me as if I was precious cargo and truly wears his heart on his sleeve. I sensed every emotion that shows on his face. He has a very dangerous job, but he does it well, without making me feel inferior.

I won't predict the future, but I shouldn't push him away so much. It seems like I'm slowly chipping away at his heart every time I do it. He had already gone above and beyond to keep me safe and help me bring Gracie back. Once, we get Gracie back home, maybe we can be close friends, as long as I can keep my libido at bay.

# Chapter Eight

Exhausted, we strolled to our Suite at The Grand European Amsterdam Hotel. Liam had stayed sitting next to me the entire two-hour trip, minus when I fell asleep. I woke up and, realized he had lifted the armrest out of the way. He had wrapped his arm around my shoulders, and I was snuggled into his chest. His chest felt like home. I fit perfectly and felt like that space was made for me.

After not having held hands or snuggled with a man since I was married. I must admit, the connection had been a long-forgotten feeling. Lovely to let someone else carry your bags, ask if you're tired and want to nap. Whether you're thirsty and want a bottle of water, or if you want to lean back and put your feet up in those luxurious first-class seats.

Should I swear off men for self-preservation, or was it easier not to be in a relationship? Maybe I needed to do a little more soul-searching, because, within twenty-four hours, I was seriously conflicted with how attentive he is with me. Every time he touches me, it's like an out-of-body experience. I want to throw caution to the wind, rip his clothes off and devour his whole beautiful body with my mouth. No man in history ever made me want him so much with just the brush of a hand or a smile. The last time I threw caution to the wind, I wound up married to an abusive liar and had three kids.

Liam inserted his key card in the lock and opened the door. I entered and was astonished with its elegance. With my mouth wide open I panned the spectacular Suite. The Livingroom walls were pale gray and the grand sofas and end chairs were a lighter shade of navy which matched the drapes. The coffee and end tables were distressed silver with shiny glass tops. There were fresh white and light pink peonies in crystal vases on the sideboard in-between the floor to ceiling windows. An enormous cabinet stood against the far wall, as it most likely enclosed the television. I turned around and spied a wet bar surrounded by cabinets. Most likely to house the refrigerator and kettle.

"Which room do you want, Darling?" Liam asked from behind me as he set down the bags. His eyes followed me as I walked around, he was always watching. I was thinking I kind of liked the attention. If I didn't need to mind myself, I would jump in his arms and smother him with kisses right now.

"Whichever you don't want," I stated.

"No. I asked you because I wanted to know what *you* want, not what you would be left with. Look around and see which room you want and I'll make you some tea."

"Thank you, Liam, but English tea puts me to sleep, and we still need to eat. I'm starving."

"Aye, I'll make you a wee coffee then," He said through his crooked smile.

"Thank you," I whispered as I stopped my panning and smiled. I walked through both bedrooms and inspected them. After I retreated from mine, I pointed over my shoulder and humbly confirmed, "This Suite is unbelievable, Liam. Thank you. I'll take this bedroom over here, if that's okay?" I said as I pointed over my shoulder and smiled like a child on Christmas morning. "The bed is massive and the room has a colossal bathroom I could get lost in. There's even jets in the bathtub. I wish I had brought my lavender bath salts that would be heaven." After he deposited our luggage in our rooms and turning the kettle on, Liam sat down on the sofa and said,

"Sit with me, Darling, and we'll order our supper."

I sat down on the cushion next to him, and he automatically wrapped his arm around my shoulders and dragged me across the sofa, closer to him. I naturally leaned

my head on his shoulder without a thought as we perused the

one dinner menu for a long while. I was so comfortable I

closed my eyes. I nearly fell asleep as Liam asked,

"What kind of wine do you fancy?"

"Oh, I don't drink wine," I drawled sleepily. "I'm more

of a dark rum or tequila girl," I answered. Liam peered down

at me like I was nuts, threw his head back and laughed,

embracing me with both arms around me, he kissed the top of

my head. I didn't understand why that was funny.

"Your doormat says, I hope you brought wine."

At that, I laughed out loud and replied, "That is funny,

and wine is for the guest to drink as I can't seem to keep it in

the house. My two oldest love wine, but when my girlfriends

come over, we make cocktails. Other than that I don't usually drink."

"Aye. Would you like a wee cocktail," he inquired, still smiling.

"Sure, two Captain and cola's, heavy on the Captain. Oh, with a lime wedge, please. A full wedge, so I can squeeze it, not a slice."

"I may wear a pirate leg, but I'm more of a Scotch man, Aye," Liam said.

At that, I laughed out loud and shook my head looked up at him, and explained, "Silly man, I wasn't being polite, I know what I like, and they're both for me as I'm not driving anywhere, *and* the waiter won't need to come back. I need to relax or I'll never sleep tonight." I informed him. Liam shook his head, dislodged me from my spot, and stood. He stretched his arms up over his head and yawned, walked to the room's phone and ordered our dinner, and added an extra meal for Kian who guarded the hallway. He handed me my coffee and sat back down, snuggled me back into my new favorite spot.

"Where do you stay when you come here to visit Grace," he inquired.

"I rent a nice canal boat not far from here. It's cozy and Gracie loves it. She stays there with me, or my other girls and Kylie if they come. She's one of my girls. We work on our catch and release, then take walks around the Amstel and hit the cute shops."

"Wait, you fish," Liam questioned.

"Sure, we all do. I bought a house on the Lough, remember. That was not by accident. Did you miss my fish cleaning station out back? My parents are huge sport fishermen, so was my Grandpa. Not Grandma, though, she only cleaned our catch so Grandpa could fry the fish up in the turkey fryer. Big family fish fries with cornbread and cold draft are the best. Mom has nine brothers and sisters, and they all come with my cousins and their children.

"Lilly's Godfather, who is also my uncle Branden by marriage, is a huge sport fisherman too. He's got more mounts in his house than I think anybody should. Last time I was there, I counted thirty. I don't see how my Aunt Maryanne puts up with his taxidermy bill.

Grandpa used to fly me to the lake and take me out in his boat to his favorite fishing spot when I was younger. He swore me to secrecy to only talk to my Mom and Uncle about his spot. He said they were the only other ones that he shared it with. He pulled out these two and three-foot-long pike like it was nothing. Netting them in I'd bonk them on the head with the baseball bat. Then he would use his chained glove to get the hook out. The entire top of their mouth is full of barbed teeth and terribly dangerous if they're not stunned. I have the best memories of my Grandparents.

"My parents used to take me and my brother on Salmon runs on the big water. We had this special spot we would go to and every year, like clockwork, we would pull out one after another. Mom always caught her and Dad's limit first. She is the best fisherman next to Grandpa and my uncle. Within a few hours, we would all catch our limit. Dad would drive the boat back to our campsite, and we'd swim while Mom cleaned all the fish and packed them in the ice cooler."

"You camped too?" Liam asked

"Well yeah, I'm sure you have too. Maybe we could have a little competition sometime to see who can set up camp faster. I think my best time was five minutes with a four-man tent, awning, tarp, and tent stakes included. Every now and again, we stayed up late and watch the Northern Lights or make s'mores on the campfire." I told him, and smiled in reminiscence.

"Do you ever fish or hunt?" I questioned. Liam got a smirk on his face and I said, "Oh God, no. Do not answer that." We had a good laugh. "Liam, what did you do growing up with your family?

"My Dad was a Constable for Police Scotland in Glasgow and my mam was a Math's teacher at my Primary School. My Mam is from Belfast, and they met while she was at University in Glasgow. I dinna know how she did it, five boys, a husband who was gone often. Yet, she still worked. You learned quickly to stop fooling about and mind yourself. My mate Peter, my brothers, and I used to drive her mad with our nonsense.

"Back when my Dad worked nights, my older brother, Niall, lifted his extra Constables' uniform. We walked around town behind him pointing his finger and yelling at kids to get off the street. We yelled at a pissed man, flat out in front of the pub. Yelling at him to scoot before his wife caught word, turned out, he knew who we were. Our parents, of course, found out, and we each got our arses' paddled for that one. But it was worth it." Liam admitted chuckling.

"Once a year, we would drive to the Theme Park and my parents would give us each twenty quid and wave goodbye. We caused all sorts of mischief stealing prizes and candy floss, when the attendants weren't looking. We tried to bribe the pretty lassies with them to kiss us," he said smiling. "We'd say we had to shift to the front of the line; our Mam passed out on the ride. Everyone moved out of the way every ride. We rode every ride in that Theme Park one year," he said laughing.

"We stole my mam's first brand-new car one night when I was about thirteen. Niall drove all the way to the parkway at the river. He was screaming at my brother Pat, who didn't pay attention and dropped his fag on the new seat. He drove straight into the water. We all got out alright, but our arses' were beet red for a week. We didn't see daylight for the rest of the summer. There're barriers up now, so no one else does it."

"Your poor mother. I would've beat your asses too!" I exclaimed and Liam and I roared in laughter.

A knock sounded at the door, Liam jumped up, hand on his weapon, walked to the door. After checking the peephole, he opened the door for the room service cart. He handed Kian a plate and utensils in the hallway. I put the dishes on the small table, so we could eat and poured myself and Liam fresh coffee.

"Wow, that was fast," I said.

"Well, I suppose when you rent the whole top floor of the hotel they tend to shift you to the front of the line," he said and nodded.

"You know, Liam, I can pay you for all of this. All of it, even the jet fuel and the hours for your staff. I don't expect a free ride, you know. I have savings." Liam bunched his eyebrows and put his fork down without taking the bite.

"You don't have to pay for anything, Darling. I would gladly spend every pound I have to keep you and your girls safe".

"But you don't even know us all yet. We're kind of a package deal". I said. "I want to give you this, Rose. You're not paying for anything." After a few moments of silence, while we ate, I spoke up again after swallowing the bite of my delicious blue cheese and caramelized onion hamburger and chips. I looked at him smiling and snickered at myself with what I was about to say. "Thank you, for everything. And not to be a freeloader, but does that mean we can have your employee discount so my girls to take the self-defense course this summer?" We both roared in laughter then he replied, "As you wish, Beautiful".

We didn't talk about money anymore while we finished dinner, though, Liam talked about more of the funny things about his family, his brothers and nephews in Glasgow. His nephews were teenagers and play football. He was so proud of them and their biggest fan. He always tried to catch their matches when he was home. He clearly loves them all dearly. He told me about his best friend Peter, and how they were best friends since primary school. They go on motorcycle trips twice a year through Europe. This summer, they're riding through Austria and Southern Germany. I'm so glad he has that. Lifelong friends are hard to come by, thankfully, I have several.

"Have you ever been to Glasgow?" he asked.

"Yes, I flew to Glasgow for my friends' wedding many years ago," I said. "Her husband was from there. It was so beautiful and very expensive. She had a ton of Swarovski Crystals on her dress and looked so stunning. Too bad it didn't work out for them, but they got a few great kids out of it." I advised him as we laughed.

When we finished or dinners, and I was into my second cocktail, Liam pulled out his phone and put on one of my favorite slow country songs. He placed his phone on the table and stood, leaned down and held out his palm to me he asked,

"Would you dance with me, please?" I smiled, took his hand and stood, tentatively placing my left hand on his shoulder, right hand embraced in his between us. He bent his head down where his forehead touched mine, and he looked into my eyes and smiled shyly. I was so nervous, I could feel that I was blushing. I could tell he was nervous too as his body trembled a bit as our bodies touched. I could hardly breathe when he was holding me. I couldn't keep my eyes open, I was so overcome with passion for this man. If he kissed that magic spot on my neck, I might swoon right here.

After a bit, we laughed, danced, and sang through about five or so of our favorite slow songs while he dipped and twirled me in and out, in dramatic fashion. In and out as I evaded his mouth. As I casually turned my face away from his, I could feel his hot breath on my neck. His breathing was as ragged as mine. He can belt out the tunes like a pro. He was distracting me it worked. I thanked him for the dances, gave him a quick kiss on the cheek, and said goodnight.

I can't think of him like this right now. No matter how good he feels. I must focus on getting Gracie back.

After my evening routine, I laid in bed and tried to distance myself from the looming pressure between both Liam's attention and Gracie's rescue. I checked my social media on my tablet and had a few laughs. I can't listen to music in bed, it ramps me up too much. I opened my reading app and began to read a vampire novel I had earmarked. Normally, I wouldn't read that genre, that's more Graces thing. I couldn't dare read a romance, thriller, or crime drama.

After relaxing more, I finally put it away and prayed for God to keep Gracie from harm and bring her home.

# Chapter Nine

Sunday Morning I showered and dressed for my day. As I walked to the wet bar to make coffee, Liam greeted me with hugs from behind and gave me several feather-light kisses my neck in just the right spot. Closing my eyes, and moaned as I enjoyed it, as it overwhelmed my body and mind for a moment. I can't lead him on. All this between us must stop. Maybe when we're back, I'll accept his dinner offer. *Maybe.*

Fresh coffee in hand, I turned to hand him his, and stopped dead. He had his shirt off and I nearly had a mini orgasm right there. My heart palpitated and my breathing loud and erratic. After I saw his huge hairy chest, I turned crimson. He gave me a crooked smile, and let go of me walking to the breakfast laid out on the table. I had to stop and compose myself before I moved. Not sure if I had to change my panties or not, I started counting in my head as I tried to slow my breathing. One Mississippi, Two Mississippi.

How can one man affect me in such a way? Seven years is one hell of a long time, definitely the longest dry spell of my life. It feels like I'm in high school again getting butterflies, because my new crush asked me to the school dance. He strutted himself to the table with his shirt off like a hairy beast, as if he didn't see my reaction. No. He *caused* my reaction. *The beast did that on purpose.*

I noticed he had athletic shorts on. Before I thought better of it, I said,

"Hey, let's see that bionic leg."

"Bionic leg," he questioned smirking.

"Yeah, I have a bionic ear and you have a bionic leg. I'll show you mine if you show me yours." I challenged with one eyebrow lifted and a small smile.

Liam sat at the table and stretched out his left leg. It was a trans-tibial prosthetic lower calf, ankle, and foot made of black metal and was wicked as hell. I set my coffee down, and knelt in front of him, sitting on my legs. Stroked my hand down the makeshift calf down to the ankle, I felt the framework with my fingers. It had a stabilizer rod running through the middle, for support. What struck me the most was the shape. The exterior appeared as if it was almost webbed, with an angled weave. The angles weren't sharp, they were curved but acute. The prosthetic felt slightly textured and smooth. It had the appearance of a really cool space-age armor from a SCIFI movie.

I tapped Liam's other knee and said, "Show me the other leg." He brought his other leg out from the side of the chair. I moved both legs together, so they were parallel and held the two, stroking my hands down them to feel the muscle definition. Amazed, I told him, "The frame is identical to your other calf, ankle, and foot. Aside from your sleeve above, you would never guess you had a prosthetic. I already knew, though. My cousin wears one, and it changes your gait. He lost his in a bike accident." I looked up at him, I said, "This is sexy as hell, Liam. You're like the bionic man and terminator combined. Can you leap tall buildings in a single bound?" I inquired with a huge smile. "If you ever want to talk about it, I'm here."

Liam laughed at that and shook his head. I patted both of his knees in approval and stood. Liam took my hand, weaved his fingers in mine, with a crooked smile and said,

"I showed you mine. Show me yours." Liam stood from the table and looked at me as I turned away from him. I brushed my hair aside to show him my bone-anchored hearing device snapped to my head. I reached back with both hands and unsnapped it from the abutment and held the small brown box out for him to see. He took it and inspected it between his fingers.

Liam muttered something I could somewhat hear, but not understand. I held up my index finger for him to wait. I turned my side for him to watch me and lifted my arms to move my hair aside. But instead, Liam lightly brushed my hair over my other shoulder and grazed his fingers over my neck. It made me tremble and my eyes rolled back into my head.

After I grounded myself breathing, I snapped it back on. I told him to wait one more minute, by continuing to hold up my finger. After my bionic ear chimed as it connected, I put down my finger, turned to him and said,

"OK, sound's back now. I could hear you, but I couldn't understand you." Liam nodded but had his brows furrowed.

"Is that drilled into your skull? Is that a cochlear?" I sat down at the table and proceeded to dish up my breakfast as I explained.

"No. She's a bone-anchored hearing aid. She transmits vibrations through my skull and my left inner ear picks up the vibrations as she translates them. Over the last twenty odd years, I bought quite a few different ones, but this works the best for me.

"I can't pick up voices behind me very well, but this is digital. She's programmed to capture, from the front and the side, for my preference. The cafe is where I find I need it most. As of today, I'm entirely deaf in my right ear and going deaf in my left. My cochlea died in my right ear nearly thirty years ago, after I had a corrective operation. The specialist implanted a prosthesis in my middle ear. The surgery was successful, but I was one of the lucky two percent that lost their cochlea. The only way to fix my left ear is to undergo another surgery and is not wise for me. In the past ten years, I already, lost over half of the hearing in my left ear. In time, I will go entirely deaf, but then I will require a cochlear to be embedded. I can't have any MRI, or it will rip the prosthetic out of my head.

"My condition is called nerve deafness which is accelerating from a complex inner ear disease. The disease is genetic and most of the women in the family all hard of hearing. Thankfully, my girls haven't shown any signs yet. I read lips to pick up the gap in one's speech from the nerve deafness. She's programmed with a delay to help mend the gaps, but I still read lips. My specialist says that probably won't ever end," I explained.

"Can you turn it up to cavesdrop on the neighbors?" Liam asked smiling.

"With my first one I could, but unfortunately no, I can't turn her up. I can change channels. She's programmed with one channel to minimize background noise. I prefer quiet restaurants instead of bars or other loud places. She is Bluetooth enabled, so I can pair it with my phone, tablet, or car. I can also loop her in with at the Movie Theater. Is your com Bluetooth," I questioned.

"Aye," Liam replied.

"Are they bone conductive?"

"I didn't buy those, so no."

"They're like ten grand each. The secret service uses them, or did use them years ago, so they can't be hacked by super spies."

"Aye. You refer to it as she?" At this, I smiled and began,

"I named her Shelby. My mom found a conch shell on the beach in Florida one summer on vacation. She kept on the hall table when I was little, and I named it Shelby. I used to hold it to my ear, thinking it captured the sound of the ocean. The shape of your cochlea is similar to the inside of a seashell."

Liam smiled and shook his head, but didn't comment further on Shelby. Maybe I scared him with the mention of being deaf in the future.

I sat with Liam and ate breakfast. I had to distract myself from his hairy muscled chest. I could barely make eye contact. The way his fine dark hair swirled up to his collarbone was hypnotizing. His shorts hung low and left nothing to the imagination as to what was at the finish line of his happy trail. If this was how men reacted to a woman's breasts, no wonder they couldn't stop staring. I had to cross my legs. My pulse had gone south. "How old are you Liam?"

"I'm fifty-two. Do I look fifty-two," he asked with his eyebrow cocked and a smug smile.

I had only seen my dad or Grandfathers with their shirts off at that age. They were always in shape, but not like this. Ciaran was only forty-one when I left him and unless he was dressing, or we were having sex, he was always wearing a tee shirt. I cleared my throat and answered him, "No. Do you work out a lot?"

"Aye, I just finished. Would you like me to put my shirt on?"

"No, no you're fine." *I'm saving this for later.* "Do you listen to music when you exercise?"

"I used to when I ran, but not anymore. I use our gym at Kerberos. I'm usually there at 0600 hours with everyone else. My employees and I wind up chatting, so it defeats the purpose."

"Do you employ many women?"

"Aye, I have quite a few. In fact, Opal and Lilly's Security Teams are only women. I thought with their ages, they would be more comfortable."

"I didn't think about that. Lilly's old enough she wouldn't care, but Bee might."

"Bee," he smiled and wondered aloud. I smiled and explained.

"Yeah, my little honey bee. I bought her a necklace when she was about five. The pendant was of a little honey bee and its body was a small opal. She wore it all the time and was constantly running around outside smelling and picking me flowers. She was a tomboy for quite a while. Putting her in a dress or anything other than sweats was a feat in itself."

"What do you call your other girls?" He asked me with anticipation and a huge smile on his face. I knew he hadn't had children, but he had his nephews. Maybe he *could* relate.

"Grace is my Sunshine. I used to sing her the song while I rocked her to sleep when she was little. She had the lightest blonde hair, just like Lilly. In old pictures, I'm the only one that can tell them apart. When she smiled, she lit up the room. She was a tomboy too. She practically lived in a tree out back for years, engrossed in books. She's always been introverted.

"While Bee was catching frogs with the neighbor boys, Gracie would be in her own world, living through fantasy fiction. She has a wild imagination, though. She wrote a sixty page composition on the description of an old derelict house beyond its rusty metal gate. She won an award for her writing on that one."

\#

Once we were done with breakfast, Liam thankfully showered and dressed and the Beards joined us to go over today's agenda. "Riley and Kenneth completed reconnaissance last night at the Van Gough Museum. They secured several hidden wireless cameras around the front and back of the Van Gough as well as the Stedelijk Museum. This operation is small, so I won't be breaking it down in stages." Liam said as he pointed to each building on the Large Screen TV as he continued the Briefing.

"Mission Goal: Rescue Grace Kelly

"Plan A: At 1900 hours Kian and Kenneth will take sniper positions above the Stedelijk and Van Gough Museums with Owen as spotter. Riley and Evan and I will be out of sight on the Museum Green behind the Museums. Rose will be at the green bin, behind the Van Gough to receive Grace in exchange for the painting. Once the exchange is done, Rose and Grace will walk to the Rover on the Green, then proceed for EXFIL."

Liam followed up with Plans B and C and somewhere in there, I got lost. I understand the strategy, but the whole way through, I just stand in the same position and do the same thing. I wasn't sure how these men can take this stress. I was overwhelmed with information. All I wanted was my daughter back, unharmed, and their plans all seem like they should work. I was mistaken assuming that I was the master planner, these men had me by a long shot.

"Rosie, you got all this," Liam asked.

"Yes, yes I do." *No, not really.*

We ate late lunch from room service with the Beards. Riley and Liam used to work together often in the SAS. I learned he was from Birmingham and was exceptional with explosive devices, and from what I inferred, he is Liam's right-hand man. Kian was formerly an Irish Defense Force Ranger from Limerick, Owen was the same, but from Donegal. Their specialty, like Riley and Liam's, was Counter-Terrorism and Hostage Rescue. Evan was from Belfast and also former SAS, however, he only worked with Riley for a short time prior. His experience was Counter-Terrorism as well. Kenneth was from Essex and former SAS, and had the same specialty as Evan. It was nice to meet the Beards on a more personal level. No one touched me this time. I think Liam may have had a word with them after the Armory.

After lunch, the Beards left and Liam and I sat on the balcony. He wrapped an arm around my shoulders as we gazed at the old city skyline and watched the canal boats slowly go by below on the Amstel.

"Rosie, are you alright with the plan," Liam asked.

"Yes, but I don't think this is going to be a quick exchange. My gut tells me this is too easy, that there will be trouble, or something will go wrong." Liam looked down at me and said,

"That's why we make back up plans, Dearheart. Plans don't always go as they're supposed to. Not bringing Grace for trade is our biggest concern next to your safety. You'll have five Operatives covering you at all times. Promise me, you'll do everything as we planned?"

"Of course I will, but her being safe is my main concern. I'm expendable. Liam, can you give me a handgun?"

Liam's brows scrunched together in disbelief. Leaning back a little, he glanced down at me and said,

"What?"

"Will you give me a handgun, please?"

I looked at Liam who had a look of disbelief on his face said,

"What concerns me is that you believe you are expendable. In no way is that true. Nothing will happen to you, period. You'll have five sets of eyes on you the whole bloody time. This isn't and won't be a suicide mission, Rose. Just exchange the painting for Grace, that's all you need to do."

"I must get Gracie back. My children are everything to me. I will not give over the painting if Grace isn't there. Roles reversed, and I was in their shoes, I wouldn't bring Grace. I'm not afraid to die, Liam. I'm good with God, and all that, but I will not let them leave without giving me Grace. What about the handgun?"

Liam's eyes bugged out of his head, and he officially lost it. Abruptly standing he held his open palms out and yelled while his full Scottish accent blared,

"Sweet Jaysus, Rose, there isnae need for you to wear a gun nor are you Approved Official to carry! Six of us will be armed to the teeth with four sniper rifles between their peepers!" Angry, Liam illustrated used two fingers and pointed to his eyes.

"They nae gonna hurt ye, they just want the painting. Do you even know how to shoot?"

"Yes, my parents started teaching me when I was nine. My mother was an instructor. I prefer a .357 revolver, but a .9 mm will do just fine for my hand as long as it doesn't bite. I knew I should have asked for one in the Armory."

"No need today. Maybe next time, Aye". Visibly agitated, he clenched his jaw, and shot fire from his eyes, Liam turned and went back inside our Suite to talk to his men.

Thirty minutes later, with nowhere to go but jump in the disgusting canal from five floors up, I wiped away my silent tears. I need to get my daughter back. Liam is my only Ally right now, and the Dutch Police aren't an option. I stood and slowly walked into the Suite spotting Liam at the table, going over the map with The Beards. I gave him a small fake smile and nod, and went to my bedroom. Sitting down on the huge, wonderful magic bed and opened my tablet to the fantasy fiction I started last night. *That date isn't happening now, mate.*

Three chapters in, Liam knocked and came in. He sat on the bed, and rested his head on the backboard and kicked his legs up. He side-hugged me and kissed the side of my head.

"I'm sorry yelled, Darling, I shouldn't have." After a long pause, I still looked across the room. Choosing my words carefully and I calmly spoke,

"Liam, I understand I frustrated you with what I said, but it is important to me that you keep your cool. Every time. Yelling is a trigger that makes me pull into myself, and want to run away. I don't ever want to feel as if I need to run from you, Liam, but today I did. I have had anxiety problems most of my life. I've had a lot of bad shit happen. I need to control my environment at all times. I need to look at all outcomes before I do something big, and believe me this is not just that, it's frigging huge." I branched out my arms to demonstrate the size.

"I'll be standing there, in the middle of the night, with four walkways headed toward me and my back to at least one. That, in itself, overwhelms me. It opens the door for someone to grab me. The more prepared I am, the more confident I will be. I'm the team goldfish out there with broken ears. If anything happens that is unexpected, I won't be able to communicate with you.

"Anxiety is a real thing that I live with every day. I worry about being hurt by a stranger every time I leave the house, and I worry more about preventing it. I have to talk this out. I will choose to talk about it instead of yelling every time. You can work through almost anything if you communicate respectfully, but when one party doesn't, the breakdown begins. I appreciate every single thing you have done for me, but yelling is a full stop for me." From the corner of my eye, I saw Liam sadly hang his head.

I turned my body to Liam and prepared him for the next blow.

"Now, I need to talk to you about my history and dress-downs."

"I dinna dress you down nor would I ever." He said defiantly in his defense with his brows drawn together in disbelief.

"No, you didn't, but I need to tell you something that I keep very private. I don't share it with just anyone, so consider yourself one of the few." I looked at him directly in the eye, took a cleansing breath and continued.

"I lived with a very violent man for twenty years. He was a screamer and dress-downs were his forte. His dad was retired military, so he knew exactly how to do it. I understand that your professional world is much different from mine. I understand that a huge part of your job is to keep your men in line. They must follow your command for everyone's safety. Not only that, but to keep them alive."

Gently, I placed my hand on his and continued, "I am asking you never to do it within earshot of me or my girls, that's all. I'm not threatening you, I'm only advising you how our clocks tick. I'm sorry. I should have told you before about the dressing down yesterday, when I realized what you do. I didn't think. It may seem trivial to some, but this is a high priority for me and my girls. Think of it this way, would you ever yell at your siblings or nephews like that?"

"No, of course not. My brothers yes, but not the wee ones. Nobody should do that and I'm sorry for yelling at ye. I was out of line, you really shocked me with what you said is all," he admitted lifting his palm up. After a beat, he continued,

"I do yell too much. I do not even think about it. My entire career has involved yelling or being yelled at as a standard form of communication. Whether you're reporting to your superior, or on the battlefield. My heads wrapped up in getting Grace back, Rose. It's not to excuse for me yelling, but I am in work mode. I won't yell at ye again, I promise, Darling. I'm sorry." He said and rubbed his other hand on my knee.

"You didn't know, Liam. In every other world, you had a normal reaction. I used to scream all the time before I got married. If you asked my mother, she'd say it was my strong suit. I'm wired differently now, is all. My marriage changed me and I had to learn to communicate in another way as a result. I still lose it, but I do make every effort not to. I'm asking you to make that effort. If you feel like you're going to blow up, just walk out of the room and compose yourself. I won't fault you for it." Liam pulled me over to him, enveloped me in his arms. I didn't want him to let go. I enjoyed the comfort in his arms too much. After a few minutes, broke the embrace, sat back on my knees and told him,

"My friend, Emma hits a heavy bag when she gets mad. You'd never know it, but she's an angry little thing at 4'10", and only 98 lbs." I started to chuckle with the thought and continued, "She always wears these sky-high heels, from her stripper job so she can reach stuff. I used to ask her if she had to wear them, so she could reach the bag at the gym." I said as we smiled and giggled.

"Are we alright?" Liam asked me with his sad puppy dog eyes.

"Yea, we're more than alright, and thank you for listening to me and apologizing. It means so much to be heard. I wasn't heard for two decades. Liam, will you give me a gun?" He shook his head and said,

"I'm not giving you a gun, Rose. You willna need one. Do you think your husband is involved in this?"

"He's dead, Liam," I stated reassuringly and patted his knee. Not wanting to begin that conversation now, I deflected. "I'll tell you what, it's already past 4 pm and I'm wound pretty tight, I'm going to take a hot bath in that huge jet tub before dinner and relax while you guys do your thing."

"Hold on. Wait here one minute, I got you something," he said as he stood from the bed.

Two ticks later, Liam appeared with a box of lavender bath salts.

"I had Riley pick that up for you in the shop downstairs. You said you wished you had some for the bath here," he confessed as he held them out to me and gave me his sheepish grin.

Completely floored, I was speechless. He actually listened to me. I couldn't write him off. *And* he was going above and beyond to help me get Grace back. I thanked him and gave him a big hug, and a quick kiss on the cheek, running to the bathroom before my tears fell. Silently, I thanked God he hadn't inquired more about my late husband. I should refer to Ciaran as my late husband by now. I went about my hot bath with bath salts and hairband love songs playlist. Next time, I'd make sure they were non-foaming bath salts before I turned on the jets.

# Chapter Ten

After my relaxing bath, I put my lotion on and pulled on my

socks to keep my feet soft. Still in the hotel's bathrobe, I dried

my hair with the towel. I turned off my playlist and everything

was so quiet without Shelby anchored. The calm before the

storm, I guess. I opened the bathroom door when

instantaneously, a colossal man lunged at me thrusting me to

the floor. I hit my head on the tile floor and the air in my lungs

immediately vanished.

"Where is it?" He demanded above me, fists at his

sides. "Where is it?"

I turned over on my side, gasped for breath, and

looked around for anything I could hurt him with. Nothing.

Not even a toilet brush. I rolled onto my knees and attempted to stand. I used the toilet to help lift myself, and moved forward to the counter top, placing my palms on it to stabilize myself. Without knowing if this man was from Ciaran's past, or if he wanted the painting, I questioned, "What do you want?"

"Where's the fucking painting!" He roared in my face as he bent over me, and his spittle hit my skin. I grabbed the open bottle of salicylic acid facial toner that was on the counter, and quickly raised my right arm, and squeezed it in his eyes. He grabbed his eyes and yelled, "You fucking bitch!"

He punched me in the center of my chest so hard, I lost traction in my socked feet. I propelled backward and hit my head on the exterior tile of the bathtub. Out of breath again, I curled to my stomach as I tried to seize air. I slowly brought my knees-up and attempted to crawl away from him to the other side of the bathroom. He snatched my ankles and yanked me toward him faster than lightning on the cold tile floor.

"Where is it?" Hc screamed as he pulled my ankles on my prone body. I tried to stop him, but no traction was to be found as I used both arms and legs kicking and screaming with every ounce of strength I had in me.

"I'm going to kill you!" He yelled red-faced as dropped to his knees and slithered up my body as he spun me over, jumping his groin on my hips, with such force, I gasped for air again. He leaned over and locked his meaty hand around my neck and pushed his weight onto it. I couldn't breathe. I arched my back and tried to shift him off balance. I jutted my knees-up and thrashed my arms about. I tried to punch his throat, scratch his face, and poke his eyes to no avail. Spots danced in my eyes as I began to disassociate from myself.

The last thing I clearly recalled seeing was him as he drew his arm back. His fist, had the middle knuckle out. I knew who he was immediately. He shouted, "You stupid bitch!" Right before his fist made impact, I heard a loud cough, as he fell over on top of me.

Within seconds Liam was with three of the Beards and pulled the man off of me. As I tried to reclaim my breath, Liam knelt beside me. He swiftly covered my partially exposed body with my bathrobe. He used his hands as he clinically checked my covered body all over for broken bones. After he satisfied himself that I was intact, he sat on the floor, pulled me to his lap, cradled me, and kissed my head. I gripped the front of his shirt weakly, with the strength left in my sore hands as he continued to comfort me.

Liam said something and the Beards took the man away. I didn't cry, didn't sniffle, and didn't talk. *I didn't feel, anything.*

After Liam rocked me for a long while, he spoke. Or at least, that was the first time, I realized he spoke.

"Let's stand and put you in the bed. I'll check your throat and the rest of you."

With that, I slowly moved off Liam's lap to my knees and stood. I held out my hand for Liam.

"You shouldn't be helping me, I should be helping you," he said. I lifted my hand and wriggled my fingers, and he accepted my hand and I pulled him up. Ouch! That hurt my chest. He must have seen my grimace, because he said,

"I'll fetch you some ice and be right back, Rose."

Once I stepped to the bedroom, I perched myself on the bed, and rested back on the headboard, I gently swung my legs up as my hips and lower back throbbed. Liam came back with a big bag of ice and several hand towels. He checked my body from the back of my head to the tips of my toes. He placed a towel with ice on the back of my head and one on my breastbone and knee.

He kept muttering I'm sorry over and over and kissed my head while his eyes filled with unshed tears. He tried to place some ice on the side of my neck, but I swatted it off. He handed me a cola and I gladly drank, taking small sips. My throat felt like I swallowed thumbtacks. Finally, he just held me and I held him back. After a bit, I painfully turned my neck the best I could, looked up at him and said,

"Thank you, Liam. Thank you for stopping him."

"This my fault. He should never have gotten in here. We came out of Briefing and Kenneth was gone. We found him passed out in the maid's closet down the hall. By the time we carried him back here, I heard him screaming at you in the bathroom. He was trying to kill you." He said running his free hand over his face and his breath hitched. He appeared so distraught. I just nodded and calmly said,

"Yes, he was in my dreams for at *least* the last ten years too, and right before he punches me, I wake up every time. You stopped my nightmare, Liam. Thank you." Instead of taking the "thank you", Liam stood up dislodging me from my snuggle spot. He stood at the side of the bed visibly angered, and argued.

"Thank me? Thank me? You almost died in that bathroom! Look at yer throat. Look at yer chest, Rose. See what he did to ye! If I had done my job properly, ye wouldna have ten ice packs covering ye! Look at yer neck for God's sake, Rose." Liam ran his hands through his hair in frustration, and paced the floor with his face bright red in fury.

The Scottish accent came grating out, and he was *pissed.* I sat up on my knees on the bed and winced, in an attempt to convince him of his false guilt.

"Liam, I was strangled more times than I can count. I have had black eyes, broken bones, and more concussions than I ever cared to count! My husband punched me in the head so many times that my head hurt for an entire year. An entire year! I don't care about physical pain. Jesus that was the easy part! It's not your fault! Take the fucking thank you, Liam!" I begged with my hands in fists out in front of me, I raised my voice in frustration at his stubbornness. He couldn't possibly believe this was his fault.

Liam looked at me horrified, with his mouth agape. Yes, I broke my own rule and yelled, I didn't want to tell him about Ciaran, but I had to make him understand. I was so angry! I had not attacked him, I only needed him to accept my gratitude.

Liam turned and stomped out of the room, violently he slammed the door in his wake. I sat angrily on the bed for a while and sobbed in fury at the situation. After my wet anguish was properly expelled down my face; I defiantly, got up off the bed and sat at the dressing table to inspect my new war wounds. I opened my bathrobe, and caught the first glimpse of myself. The bruises were bad. They had only just started, yet the worst I ever had.

*I can see why he's so angry now.*

They were much more spectacular than Ciaran's bruises ever were. Maybe Ciaran didn't really want to kill me, back then, like he said. No, Ciaran chose his actions. Ciaran chose to be violent.

This *was* a close one. I begrudgingly took another shower to remove the blood, and what I hoped wasn't brain matter off of me. I washed and brushed my hair under the shower twice to make sure I removed it all. In the bathroom, I realized all the blood was cleaned and the bathmat was gone. I cautiously dressed and took two paracetamol for pain. The goose egg on the back of my head was still bad, but I planned to keep the ice on it until tonight. I needed a nap. My adrenaline vanished and now exhausted, I laid down on the bed for a short while as I iced my goose egg.

When I woke up, fresh tears streamed down my face. It's not the first time, I cried in my sleep, but hopefully it will be the last. Liam was lying on the bed and faced me, as he stroked my damp hair. I peered over at him and whispered,

"Hey."

"Hey," he whispered in reply.

"I'm sorry I yelled at you, Liam."

"I'm sorry I yelled and walked out on you, Rose."

"I told you to walk out. I shouldn't have made a rule that I can't follow myself," I said with a small smile. "I appreciate you, Liam. I'm thankful you're here to help me bring Gracie back, and I'm so grateful that you stopped him. I'm thankful God brought you into my life and I'm sorry. I'm so sorry, I pushed you away." I said and the silent tears started to fall again. Liam hugged me close with one arm, and cradled my head in his other hand while I cried. I finally cried. Hallelujah. It all came out as I clung to him as my lifeline. He never asked again about my ex-husband, although, I understood I shocked him with my confession. After a bit, he needed to work on another project for Sheelagh and left me. I laid there lost in thought.

He was not like my past abusers. He listened to me, comforted me and saved me repeatedly. He was my protector and my other half. I don't want to live my life without this man. I had been as foolish as I pushed him away. It was then, I made up my mind. I need him. I'd waited for him my whole life and I've made up my mind. When Gracie comes back and things die down, I will tell him. *He's mine and I'm not letting him go.*

#

I walked into the Living-room of our suite and noticed all the Beards, but Liam was gone. They all hung their heads in shame. I looked up at each one of them as delicately said, "Thank you, for rescuing me. You weren't the cause of this. He made his choices, and somehow, he would have found another way in. I'm thankful you all are here to have my back and help bring Gracie home. Now, please join us for dinner. I'd like to know all of you better, since most of you have seen me half-naked." I said with a small smile, trying to lighten the mood.

They all nodded with small smiles and took turns giving me gentle hugs as I stood there in my favorite glitter tee shirt and jeans. Riley told me that Liam had already ordered dinner, before he had his next meeting, and it should be here soon. I sat on the sofa and closed my eyes as my head ached.

Liam came out of his bedroom shortly after and sat down on the sofa snuggling next to me. He turned on the TV and changed channels to the National news.

I kissed his neck, wrapped my legs under me and zoned out, snuggled into my spot on his chest, as I wrapped my arms around his firm middle. He embraced me in his arms and kissed my head as he continued to watch the news. He was mine and I fit perfectly with him. I was his missing piece as he was mine.

Evan came over and spoke to us for a while. It was nice to listen to a Northern Irish accent for a change. Sometimes, I still struggled with Liam's accent. Especially, when his full-on accent came out, and he used terms I never knew existed, like bawbag or swatched. I was sure he would be dumbstruck when I went back home and my Midwestern corn bred slang was unleashed. Since I moved to Northern Ireland, I had frequently been told my accent wasn't "thick". I began to shy away from my slang and begun to use their terminology, so they'd stop correcting me.

We relaxed and laughed over dinner on the sofas. I didn't speak or eat very much, with my throat still sore, but Liam had thought ahead. Being his attentive self, he ordered me chocolate ice-cream which went down with ease as it cooled my throat. It was so creamy and delicious. I identified Acts of Service, Quality Time, and Physical Touch as his love languages for sure.

About 9 pm the seven of us headed out to the Van Gough in two Rovers. Riley and Liam drove ours as I had the backseat to myself. I rolled my window down as far as it would go and studied the city at night. Cyclists were still about, but the city had wound down to prepare for the start of the new work week.

Once we arrived at the Museum Green, I observed the Garden's beauty. It was exceptionally quiet as all the patrons had gone home to their beds. The freshly cut grass, on the green, made it smell like summer. Yellow daffodils and red tulips colored the entrance way to the Promenade walkway. Scattered benches lined the garden for the patrons' leisure. The wind rustled the new leaves on the few dozen trees scattered about the garden. I had never been here before, but Gracie had several times.

The entire Promenade was a massive expanse and that was only the back. There were so many obstacles, between the museum and the Rover, I didn't know where to begin. Anyone could hide behind a huge potted tree, garbage bin, or art sculpture. This entire operation made my skin on my forearms and neck itch from nervousness.

Kenneth, Owen, and Kian had already climbed the rough brick museum faces to prepare their hides. Evan was out and about doing recon. Liam and I stayed in the Rover with Riley while they watched the cameras from their cell phones and chatted about the operation. While I sat, bored out of my mind, I decided to pray. Pray for my daughter's safe return and for Opal and Lilly's safety throughout this disaster, and for the Beards and Liam to come out unharmed. After my rosary, Liam peered over at me from the front seat and said, "Darling, it's time." I nodded in response and exited the Rover.

Liam was entirely in Commander bad-ass mode in his tactical vest and hat. We reviewed the plan for a final time. He hugged me, but not nearly long enough. I didn't want to let go, but I had to in order to bring Gracie back. I had to let him go, just one more time. I placed my right palm on his cheek and kissed his other cheek, right next to his mouth, and let my lips linger after as I breathed him in. We had four men watch us, so now was not the time. He looked at me and furrowed his brow. I had pushed him away for so long, he must not have expected it. He stared down at me hesitantly, nodded, and led me toward the bin. At the corner landscaping, his hand left the small of my back and I ambled to the finish line at the green bin. Alone.

Standing still, I stared down the walkway in front of me. I was directly in front of the rear exit of the museum with the drawing tube strap over my shoulder. Will Grace walk to me through there? Turning my head to the right I glanced down the walkway toward the small Van Gough Stichting building and Moco Museum. People probably wouldn't walk this way unless they'd come from the Moco or parking area, would they?

Completely exposed, I turned completely around to view the third walkway that ran in behind the Van Gough in front of the Promenade Green. The view was obstructed by the large potted trees and ramp wall that leads to the Stedelijk Museum and supermarket. This must be the way. This was the usual way people walk from the city center unless you were parking. What if they park? They wouldn't approach me on foot, would they? No, they'd want to protect themselves in their car. The location doesn't make sense. They would need to be close to their car unless they would drive *on* the walkway.

I peered over to where I had left Liam on the Green, and he was gone. I couldn't see him, Riley or Evan. That gave me unrest, but I breathed through it. Unzipping my jacket as I began to perspire in my nervousness, I closed my eyes, with the knowledge, Liam and the Beards were here to protect me, and I was safe. I steadied my breath and thought of my happy place at the farm. Lying in the cut grass as I peered up at the clouds, in search of shapes. I could hear my Grandfather's voice which calmed me in my head. *Don't worry, my Sweet Lovey. Everything will be alright.*

# Part Two

# Chapter Eleven

Liam

I gazed upon My Beautiful Rosie on the pavement, from the Promenade Green through my Spotter Scope, as she stood by the green bin. She is the most beautiful woman I've ever seen. I knew I wanted her from the first moment I laid eyes on her. She was walking down the street toward the cafe as her long auburn curls bounced off her shoulders and back as she scanned all around. Her situational awareness left something to be desired, as she brought too much attention to herself. At the least, she paid attention more than most. I'll give her that.

I asked around and found out who she was. Turned out, my self-defense instructor, Andrew, frequented her establishment regularly, as did most of my employees. I asked him to suggest taking his course and teach her how to be more aware without bringing attention to yourself. She immediately signed up for the class and, of course, I threatened to break his arms if he hurt her in any way. We had a good laugh.

Soon, I started to buy coffee at the cafe every day after work. Each time I made contact with her, she had a beamer. Not just a wee one either. She beamed bright red from her cheeks down to her breasts and smiled. Her smile was always the highlight of my day. She lit up the room like a ray of sunshine. Her eyes changed color when she smiled from sky blue to a crystal blue that shined like diamonds.

Her curves are unbelievable. She looks like a red-haired Marilyn with the way her denim and tee cling to her and accentuated that tiny waist just waiting for my hands. She would be to-die-for as a blonde. Every single touch, every look, and every time I smell her, I am spellbound. I can't get enough of her. I want to devour her until she writhes uncontrollably and screams my name. I frequently need to adjust myself just the thought. I knew from the first time she spoke to me that I wanted to spend the rest of my life with her, if she would only give me a chance.

I would do anything for her, but the concept is lost to her as she doesn't understand why. My Regiment would do anything for each other, as my men and I would today. She accepts me for what I've done and who I am without hesitation, and for that, I would do anything to keep her safe, and anything to keep her daughters safe. Anything she wanted, I would give her.

I almost lost her today. I thought I was too late when I shot that pro. Two minutes later and she'd be gone. I killed a man on top of her, and she *still* accepted me. Brain matter in her hair and half exposed she didn't even mind. I was so angry with myself I can hardly see past it.

When she told me what had happened with her husband, I was rendered speechless in shock. Tis one thing to have the knowledge of someone you are not close to but quite another when violence happens to someone you've fallen for. I didn't know what to do. I needed to process the information she just thrust at me before I did anything else. I certainly didn't want to say the wrong thing and escalate the conversation further. The argument had escalated enough already.

When I listened to her crying after I left, I felt terrible. It ripped my heart out. I understand what my leaving seemed like. It appeared as if I was angry and I left her because she yelled, but that was nowhere near my intention. She can yell at me all she wants. She had a normal reaction. Anyone would be upset. The fact that she didn't cry *hysterically* caught me by surprise. Initially, she was in shock. But after, she was too calm. She had experienced this kind of violence many times before, and *that* was the reason.

She works hard on reigning in her emotions for sure, but she needs to understand she doesn't need to around me. She can unleash her worst and I'll be there to catch her every single time. Hopefully, in the future, I will be better prepared to approach the subject. We will need to talk about her abuse again, someday, but it doesn't change how I feel about her.

The thought that her husband or anyone had hurt her makes me see red. I had a mind to dig up his corpse and dismember him just for the sake of her honor. She didna deserve what she got from him. No woman deserves that. I understand now, why she pushed me away for so long. She'd been hurt too much, and scared I'll break her heart and her body. No wonder she doesn't want the yelling. She's lived through domestic abuse and come out intact. That takes immense strength in itself.

Her behavior makes complete sense to me now. Her situational awareness, self-defense course, the huge dog, and safe room. But if her husband is dead, why is she still so anxious. Maybe she has Post Traumatic Stress. She keeps herself so close. She refuses to accept my help, which kills me. Rosie needs to prove to herself she's strong enough, that she can accomplish this on her own. She is plenty strong enough, and she doesn't even realize it.

I caught sight of the pink, purple, and teal feather tattoo wrapped around the outside of her left breast. Tiny little colored birds flew out of the loose ends. The tattoo was beautiful. She was beautiful. I wasn't sure what her ink means, but hopefully, I will earn her trust enough to tell me someday.

I thought she wanted to kiss me back there, but she didn't. No. I willna force myself on her. I invaded her space enough. She gets my goat every time she turns color and trembles. I know she wants me. I know it with everything in me. The way her body reacts to my every touch. Every time she looked at me, I sensed it. Tonight, she clung to me she never left my side. I want that forever. Forever with her by my side would be bliss.

*She is mine. She belongs with me.*

The wind picked up quite a bit and the leaves on the trees rustled. They changed from green to white as the leaves overturned in the breeze. The wind began to howl and gained strength by the minute. Owen had already clocked two silver Mercs with tinted windows circling the road in front of the museums multiple times, but no one was behind the museums on the pavement but Rosie.

She looked my way, unzipped her black leather jacket to expose her tee that said, "Crazy Motherfucker." I laughed to myself. Only Rosie would wear that tee with the crazy coated in pink glitter. She wore the craziest shirts outside of the cafe I guess her dad kept a whole collection of them. She told us tonight they make her seem closer to him while she's physically three thousand miles away.

I heard the rumble first, I looked through my spotter scope as a black motorbike sped up the pavement from the East and abruptly stopped in front of Rosie, screeching the tires. The rider wore a black helmet and leathers, keeping his identity concealed. The rider said something to her, then sped off. *Damn, I need to buy bone conductive coms.*

Rosie turned around taking off in a sprint, with the drawing tube up the steps and down the pavement between the Museums. In the wind, her long red ponytail was flying everywhere. In half a second, I clicked my com and commanded, "Principal on the run between the buildings, headed toward the primary road Paulus Potterstraat! Riley bring the Rover to the road in front of the intercept! Go!" Four clicks followed as I ran as fast as I could to Rosie. *I can always replace a fucked up prosthetic, but I can't replace her.*

Running as fast as I could, gnashing my teeth doing my best to ignore my painful stump. When I got to the Northwest corner of the Van Gough, I saw Rosie at the far end of the next street past the Moco Museum at the Underground Parking Ramp, standing next to a silver Merc. A hulk sized blonde thug fought to take the drawing tube from her.

While they continued their cock-fight, Rosie kicked and screamed. He pushed her to the ground and snatched the tube. Quick as lightning, in a move I never saw before, she grabbed his leg and clung to it wrapping her arms and legs around his and throwing her weight on his foot, preventing him from jumping back in the car. Her long hair looked like a fireball, flying everywhere in the wind.

"Where's my daughter!" I barely heard her yell from two blocks away.

Only half-way there, running towards them, I lifted my SIG and commanded, "Drop it!" I was still nearly two blocks away and I couldn't fire and possibly hit Rosie. The thug glanced up at me in panic. He reached down, snatched Rosie under the arms, and lifted her as he forcefully shoved her into the silver Merc still attached to his leg. The rear door was still open as the driver sped off. Running as fast as I was able toward the weighed down car, I shot three rounds! My bullet smashed through the rear windscreen, glass shattered blowing fragments in the unforgiving wind. Successfully, I shot a man in the back of the head, as they quickly accelerated.

Running after them down the middle of the street, I tapped my com and ordered, "They have Rose and the painting, no Grace! Riley, where's that God damn Rover! I'm nearing the Underground Car Park now!" I screamed in my com while the wind whipped against me.

I could hear Riley approach on my six as the silver Merc turned left onto the intersecting street. Still running I shot again, taking out the driver side window, but did not the driver. I couldna shoot the back window again and possibly hit Rosie. The Merc sped off in a fast clip as it rounded the next corner, red taillights shined like the devil's eyes in the dark. Riley picked up speed and drove beside me, yelling out the passenger window, "Hop in now!" I slowed and threw open the door as I jumped in forgoing the seat belt. We sped off in a fast pursuit, but they were gone.

Riley, raced down the same road, with both of us checking all the side roads as we passed. We drove all over as we scanned everywhere for the silver Merc. Crossroad after crossroads we shredded our tires in the urban jungle. An abundance of colored flags, banners, and signs for the tourists created visual chaos.

For an hour, we drove through the city center with both Rovers, but the Merc was in the wind. How did they get away so fast? Turning square after square we searched in the city full of one-way roads that defied logic. We navigated our way through a city that had a river that wound through it sixteen different ways, and it was a challenge. At least there were few cyclists about at this time of night.

In the second Rover, Evan traced Rosie's phone to the park off the main road, Van Baralestraat, not a mile from the Van Gough. Evan also discovered the Merc not far away, with two dead thugs. I did hit a second man, and obviously, they changed vehicles. Relentlessly, we searched the nighttime city streets, and finally, began our rendezvous back to the hotel for Debrief.

# Chapter Twelve
Liam

I yelled at the team to the point where the vein in my forehead might pop., but my disappointment wasn't in them, it was in myself. I tapped the speakerphone, on the first ring Sheelagh answered,

"How'd it go Boss?"

"Fucked up, that's how it went! God Dammit! How many Hades and Kore Teams do we have available right now!" I demanded with a growl. "Both Delta and Hotel Teams are available if you're looking for door-kickers; Zeus and Poseidon are also on standby, if you need air or water support, Boss," she informed me. "Send D, H, and Zeus with two Super-Medium HELO's and drones. Tell everyone to pack heavy, wheels up ASAP and I want that Crius Satellite online, yesterday! Hack all the street cams around the park at Van Baralestraat, and see what vehicle they moved to," I commanded. Sheelagh replied, "Aye, Boss," as I ended the call.

I was out of my head. I should have brought a second team to secure the road in front. Why didn't I do that and why didn't I give her a gun? What did I miss? Why didn't they bring Grace? I looked at my men and announced, "Teams D, H and Zeus will be here in three hours with HELO's. Order some food, we'll meet back here for Brief. Dismissed." The Team filed out except for Riley, who accompanied me at the table as we devised a plan to bring Rosie and Grace back to me.

After an hour, of running my hands through my hair in frustration, Riley looked over and asked

"You alright, Boss?"

I threw out my hands in frustration. "No Brother, I'm not. I should've had another Team for the front. It took four minutes! Four fucking minutes from start to finish and I lost her. I should have had the Crius Satellite online and drones in the air, I should've given her a gun, and I should have had bone conductive com to give her!" Escalating, I yelled in frustration.

"I do this for a living. I never second guess myself. I always know what I'm walking into and prepare for the worst. We've run into fire so many times, I can do it in my sleep. I could stroll through a battlefield in Afghanistan, smoking a cigar in one hand, firing an AR15 with the other, and still come out a winner! Yet, today, I couldn't save my own woman!" I yelled as I waved my arms in front of me.

I placed my hands on my hips and looked down, I broke, "I let her down, Riley, not just her, but her daughters." I pointed to myself and continued. "If I don't find her, *I* will have to tell those poor girls not just their *father* is dead, but their mother and sister are gone now too. I willna to do that. In thirty years, I have never lost a hostage. Thirty fucking years, Brother!"

I motioned toward the table and ordered, "Let's work." After a few minutes had passed I spoke again.

"If you say a word to anyone I'll rip your tongue out like that asset in Peru, but I havta bring these women back. My heid's full o' mice, and I haven't taken a breath in the last two hours. She's under my skin! She's under my skin, and she's messed with my heid. My heart's been ripped out of my chest without her here."

"What if I don't bring her back? Or, what if I don't bring her daughter back, and she then willna come near me? She infuriates the fuck out of me with the shite she says. She had a dead professional on top of her, Riley. I almost lost her today because of it, then she turned around and yelled at *me*. She yelled at me after she almost died, because I wouldn't accept her thank you! What happened then, Riley? She cried," I said with my palms up in disbelief.

I pointed to myself and added, "If I yell, it'll set her off, and she'll be crying. It was my fault she was, Riley. I broke her down. I did that." I pointed to the balcony and continued, "She was out there crying on the balcony today after I yelled at her." Putting my hands on my hips I hung my head, and shook it with remorse. I continued, "I yell for a living, you understand me. But no. No, she wants me to keep the yelling at work, or hit a God damned heavy bag.

"I won't dare begin to figure out what goes on in her heid, but she's not a daft woman. You might think it, but she's not. No. Everything she does and says has a purpose. She thinks through everything in detail, and I think *I* am a god? She's fucking Rhea. She is the goddess of the universe the way she controls things," I said as I shook my head.

"She's strong enough to be out there without me, I know it. She'll find her way out. She's planning it now, I know she is in that foolish shirt," I said with a low chuckle.

"She's a Crazy Motherfucker, Riley. She's a Crazy Motherfucker and so much stronger than she thinks. Her husband used to hit her. She said she's had more black eyes, broken bones, and concussions than she cared to remember. She's strong enough to make her way through it, but I'm nae strong enough to be here without her. I can't. I can't and I won't. I have to find her. I have to find her now. Riley, please help me find her fucking now!" I begged as I slapped my hand on the tabletop.

"Yes Sir," Riley said with his brows pinched together with the knowledge of her past I mistakenly confessed. He looked down and shook his head and continued the rescue plan.

Riley was my best mate in the Army. He grew up with an abusive father, and may have some insight. We'll cross that bridge when we get to it.

We made calls, as we looked for Helmsmeier's Base as we planned our strategy. Riley learned more about Helmsmeier's dealings with the German Mob. They were hours from having him killed. He owed them a Greek statue he had yet to acquire. He also had a £6M debt he owed them.

Helmsmeier's base was in Germany, but that didn't mean his hideout was. He must be local, or just across the border, in Germany. Sheelagh found street camera footage that revealed they changed vehicles at 12:08 am. They moved to a dark newer model Merc van, moved a kicking Rosie into the new van, and traveled north. Street cams lost sight of them off the Motorway as they lead out of the city center, but not over the bridge past Almere Poort, and not on the A12 into Germany. They're close.

The only nearby battle area was the pit, which wouldn't be safe for civilians who lived nearby, and attract too much attention. After I studied the Crius Satellite imagery for an hour, I made my decision. I called my best friend, Peter, over the border in Germany to prepare for battle.

By 0600 hours, nineteen of my Hades and Kore operatives, all former Special Forces, stood around the suite. I informed my men of our failed operation from earlier this morning. Even though, they all agreed with my earlier plan; I refused to concede that I did the right thing. I briefed my men on the plan to bring Wilhelm Helmsmeier out into the open.

"Sheelagh opened a bounty on Helmsmeier. The bounty is as follows: A £5M bounty on Wilhelm Helmsmeier's head to be brought in alive, by any means necessary." Whistles sounded from around the room.

"We anticipated only top tier professionals with that kind of quid up for hire. One hour ago he made contact. Unless he agrees to release both Grace and Rose at the Grotto, Saint-Augustine of Hippo Rectory, tonight at 0000 hours, the bounty goes up to £7M dead or alive.

"An hour ago, he accepted. He wants £6M if I want the girls alive, and agree to meet in person. That would fulfill his debt with the Mob. In the worst-case scenario, the money is ready to send, and we believe he's going underground after, until he renegotiates with the Mob. For the record, we'd rather not pay him, I prefer his head on a pike. Once *both* the women are delivered, if he dies, so be it. I'm not fuckin about," I ordered as I waved my arm.

"Mission Goal: Rescue Grace and Rose Kelly."

I pointed to the Crius satellite view of the Brewery Compound on the TV, I detailed the Battle Plan. "We'll drop in the South East field behind the Rectory and set up offensive and defensive measures around the Rectory and Brewery like last time. The Priests were made aware and plan to be in the basement, but as before, they will not stand their ground.

"Hotel: Offensive positions will be hidden in the cow paths along the South and East edges of the fields, two men each side in sniper positions. Spotters watching the other's six until intercept.

"Delta: Defensive positions will be both inside and outside the Brewery, one man at the South, West and East windows with one spotter and sniper in hide positioned on the roof with shades.

"Bravo: The defensive positions at the Rectory are as follows, positions at the North, South, and East using the stone wall as cover. One spotter and sniper in hide on the roof with shades.

"Zeus One and Two will man the drones.

"Zeus Three, Four and Cronus, will use the forest for cover, around the Grotto to recover the hostages.

"Pack your shit, eat and get your sleep in, we'll convoy at Amsterdam Schiphol Airport at rendezvous boarding HELO's at 1400 hours. Dismissed."

After the run-through of the recovery operation, I ate the fast food Charlie brought in for me. I laid down in Rosie's bed but couldn't sleep. I tossed and turned, but I only inhaled her perfume on the pillows. They smelled so good, I felt like I was snuggled with my nose in her beautiful long neck. I couldn't shut off my mind from running through every possible scenario. I was always able to shut it off. Every firefight, every battle, I could always disconnect myself.

Finally, after I used her bathroom, I glanced at the bath salts I got her on the counter. Turning on the bath with the hottest water they had I added some salts. I used my hand as I swished them around in the bathwater until they dissolved. I hadn't taken a bath since I was a wee lad at my parents, and I wasn't about to now without Rosie.

A bath with Rosie would be a lot of fun. The things I would do to turn her inside out. No, the things *I will do* to her when I bring her home to me. I turned off the water and got my mind out of the gutter. I kept the door shut and sat on the

floor as the room filled up with lavender filled steam.

Eventually, I sat back down and leaned back against the tile

wall. I removed the prosthetic from my painful stump.

As I sat there, I thought about her. She was the most

beautiful woman, and she was even more beautiful when she

was angry. Her eyes change color to a stormy blue, so

beautiful. The more I talked to her, the more I don't want to

stop. I never want to stop. She was so witty, funny and so

damn smart. She has a brilliant mind. Her problem resolution

is uncanny, no wonder she was hired to find an embezzler.

She could be a detective inspector easily if not for her hearing.

I love the way she bites her lip when she gets nervous.

The way she twirls her long hair around her fingers when she's

lost in thought. And when she laughs, I could listen to it for

hours. Her car dancing leaves a bit to be desired, and her

singing voice was awful. What I wouldn't do to hear her rap old school again, I thought and laughed to myself.

I need to keep her safe from everything. I want to wrap her up in a blanket and carry her under my arm so nothing can ever hurt her. Damn her husband. If he wasna already dead, I'd kill him myself, and it would feel *good*. She touched my prosthetic leg. She didn't even flinch and called it sexy as hell. It was as if it impressed her.

She was grand with my career, and she hadn't asked me to change it. The only thing she asks for is never to yell in front of her or the girls, which I shouldn't do anyway. She's everything I yearn for. I need to persuade her to unlock her heart to me. We would be extraordinary together. That would be heaven. Heaven on earth. She is my goddess, Rhea. The goddess of my universe.

Several hours later, I woke up on the floor. Snuggled up to her damp towel, when my mobile rang, I answered it, "Cronus."

"Sir, it's time."

I picked myself up of the floor and hung up her towel. I wanted it to be dry if I brought her back. No. *I will bring my goddess home to me.*

# Chapter Thirteen

We dropped at the Rectory right on schedule with heads on a swivel. Helmsmeier could already have his men in the surrounded fields, watching our every move, but that was doubtful. The meet at the Grotto would give us the best cover, and we would be in complete control. The plan always worked as long as they brought the hostages.

I was sure if they had watched, they could view our snipers choosing their hides with on the Rectory and Brewery rooftops, but there were no other high grounds in the area. It was too light outside to use their NVG's (Night Vision Goggles) yet to compromise our position in the forest. I clicked my com once, "Cronus, any eyes on us, over." I asked.

"Bravo Three, Negative." my spotter chimed in as my two other spotters clicked in response. "Hold positions until contact. Hold fire unless fired upon, over." I ordered, followed by four clicks.

Thank God this is just a brewery and not a distillery. If Peter ever moved the priests to the hard stuff, we'd need to find another spot like this. Peter, my best friend from primary school is the Rector, and he's always been the coolest guy known to man. I never understood why he didn't ditch me back when I joined the Army, especially when I started Kerberos. It's not as if he doesn't know what I do. He says he loves me unconditionally, and prays for my poor soul three times a day. I tell him I'll pray for his liver in return, and we always end with our full belly laughs while we finished our pints.

Once in position, we all sat in stillness until go time. I used my time to mentally pray three rosaries, as I sat in front of the Blessed Virgin. It's not as if I didn't have the time. I don't think I had ever prayed so hard, prayed yes, but that hard, no. "Please Lord, just bring them back to me unharmed. I can't say I'll stop shooting people, but I will work on my swearing. And if you could make Rosie open her heart to me, it would be appreciated. I can't be without her, Lord. Please help me. I nae ask ye for much."

Right on schedule, "Zeus One, two HELO's spotted five klicks from the target, ETA four minutes, over," chirped through the com.

"Copy Zeus One. Hold positions," I responded. Exactly four minutes later, I received the next transmission, "Zeus Two, HELO's on the ground with twelve tangos disembarked. One female in sight, I repeat, one female insight, over".

"Copy Zeus Two, hold positions." *What the ever-loving fuck is he playing at?*

I waited and patrolled the pathway until finally, the two turned the corner. Helmsmeier had an air about him that oozed pretentiousness. As he slowly strolled up the tree-covered pathway to the grotto in a black tailored suit, with his left hand around Grace's arm. He had a smug look on his face as if he was impenetrable. He had no idea how penetrable he was. I could kill him this very moment before he even had his next thought. With Grace, I wasn't sure what I expected, but a wee lassie with an electric blue pixie cut hair was not it. She had plastic-cuffs on, but seemed otherwise unharmed. *Please God, pray that be the case.*

"Where is Rose," I firmly demanded, I had not drawn my weapon yet.

"TSK, you didn't think I would be daft enough to bring them both did you," he asked with a click of his tongue. "Why would I permit you to shoot me in these woods, Liam? You're no wiser than you were ten years ago. When I blew up your inept Squadron in that convoy, I was aiming at you, Officer Commander, or should I address you as Cronus," he said with a restless chuckle.

I knew he was trying to fuck with my head. It wasn't going to work. No way was he responsible for that RPG firing. It was proven to be a faulty trigger from a green Allied Trooper, there to protect the convoy from the approaching assault we were intercepting five clicks away.

Helmsmeier laughed out loud and shoved Grace in my direction. I caught her quickly before she fell. Taking out my favorite KA-BAR from my tactical belt, I and cut off her plastic-cuffs. I asked her, "Are you alright, Grace?" She nodded but didn't speak. I rubbed where the cuffs had rubbed on her wrists and asked, "Did they harm ye?" She shook her head, no. Thank Christ. I could tell where dried tears streaked her cheeks in mascara.

"Did ye see your mother? Is she alright?" I questioned and she nodded again. Good, I'll persuade her to talk later. "Go hide behind Mary in the Grotto, pet, and shield your eyes," I instructed. Grace did as I asked and rounded the Virgin Mary eight feet behind me, got down on her haunches behind its base, and hid herself from what was to come.

In complete command now I sneered, and bared my teeth as I raised my SIG to protect Grace and demanded again, "Where the fuck is Rose, Helmsmeier?"

"Where's my money," he questioned.

"I don't see both women."

"You really don't remember me, do you, Liam? I am offended. I saw the wheels turning, and thought you had it, but I must have overvalued your intelligence," he said somberly as he shook his head.

"I looked a little greener back in those days, but I know you've thought about me every morning and night for the last ten years." He waited a beat, and continued. "Every morning when you put on that metal leg and every night when you take it off," he said as he imitated his statement waving his hand about.

"Tell me, does it still pain you? Do you get those phantom pains I read about? Better yet, do you get up in the night to piss and fall on your face, because you'd forgotten you're a cripple in your slumber?" He said, then bent over and laughed. With crazy eyes, he righted himself. "I would love to see that, Cronus falling on his face," he continued. "How do the ladies like it? I bet you don't get much ass anymore. You were always the looker before I tore open your face. You must become overheated with that thick beard. Go on, show me your leg, Liam. I must view my creation," he said with expectancy. Furiously, I ended his tirade, I raised my SIG, and centered it between his eyes and ordered.

"Last time before I blow a hole in your brain. Where the fuck is Rose Helmsmeier!"

With a smirk on his face, he locked his eyes with mine and said, "Who would have thought we would covet the same woman. I had nearly forgotten about you, with my other conquests and all. Then one day, low and behold I watched you walk into that appalling café and you toyed with that fat woman who stole my painting," he said dryly. "I wager she won't come near the monster I made you. She may smile a lot, but she'll always run."

"Truly, it is disconcerting you don't remember me, Liam. You blew up my parents in Kuwait because they were in the hotel with the Pakistani Prince and you don't even fucking remember! They weren't terrorists and you killed them! Their blood is on your hands, Cronus!" After a beat, he composed himself and continued.

"Here, let me assist your recollection. From now on, you should address me as Helms, Gefreiter, and Private First Class Will Helms." He produced a huge smile when he saw the pieces click together, and I realized my icy expression changed to a snarl. "I waited for this for so long, twenty-four years to be precise! I would love to exterminate you but watching your suffering is so much more satisfying," he said shaking his head. "I only needed one woman to obtain my prize, but thanks to you ended up with two." Then he whispered, "You'll never find you're Rose, but don't worry, I have found mine. You have twelve hours before she blows. Just like you did with my parents."

"Motherfucker!" I screamed as I pointed my gun right between his eyes, but I couldn't pull the trigger. I needed the asshole alive, so he would lead me to Rose, and he had planned on it! All hell broke loose as everything seemed to happen at once. Multiple shots rang out as Helmsmeier turned and sprinted through the woods to the clearing where his two HELO's were. I received Intel through my com,

"Shots fired! Shots fired South field! Has the package been delivered?"

"Cronus, one package is secure. Keep Helmsmeier alive, kill his men, and don't let that bird leave, over." I responded as I rounded to Grace in the Grotto and held out my hand "Let's move, lass." Grace gladly took my hand as we hightailed it down the path through the woods, and down the road to the Rectory. I ordered through my com, "Grotto detail, reposition to east edge of woods and engage, go!"

Grace followed my lead until we reached the Rectory gate when she spoke up,

"I've been here before. The Brewery is safer, come with me." Grace grabbed my hand again as she took a sharp right, and drug me across the road. If that blue hair wasn't a huge shoot me sign, I don't know what was. It looked like the leftover blue candy floss on a short stick, running on its heels from a chubby toddler at a carnival. *And I was the chubby toddler!*

Shots rang out all around us as my men created a cover. We made it inside when Peter embraced Grace in a one-arm hug. Peter and his shaggy hair had a fag hanging from his mouth, as usual, turned to Grace saying,

"Gracie, I had hoped the next time we met, it would be to buy your Granny ale, but we'll chat about that later. I'm diggin the blue hair wee one."

*Eh?*

Before I sent her down to the basement with the rest of the priests, Grace turned to me and asked,

"Do you have another gun or a crossbow? I'm better with a crossbow." Damn it all to hell, like mother like daughter. Everything in me said no, but I knelt without question. Pulling my spare Ruger .09 mm out of my ankle holster I handed it to her with two spare clips. I pulled out my spare com, turned it on, and handed it to her. She quickly placed it in her ear like a pro.

She thanked me, and after she completed the safety checks, bent down, and crawled in and out of the mash tanks to the West window. Peter looked at me like I was mad, but after I waved him off, he followed her. I went to the opposite window that faced the South field.

Throughout our sprint from the Grotto and firefight, I heard my men calling off their kills. "One down, two down, three down." Within four minutes after we entered the Brewery, all of Helmsmeier's men were dead except for one who covered the HELO, as Helmsmeier fired at us from the rear. "Eleven down," I heard through my com. Once fire stopped we waited for a beat, then two. My blood pumped so hard all I heard was my own heartbeat. A single shot fired from inside the HELO and it was all over. After checking on Grace and Peter, I loaded a new clip and walked outside.

"Cronus, approaching HELO three now, cover me." I ordered into my com and jogged outside gun up, head on a swivel, hoped Helms didn't just take his life. As I reached the HELO, I caught a glimpse of the interior cabin and knew he had. *Couldn't fly a HELO, could ye cocksucker. Outa money and outa time.*

I clicked my com and barked, "Roll call." I snatched the drawing tube from Helms bloody grasp. After all of my men chimed in I ordered into my com, "Round up all the bodies to their HELO's. Zeus Three and Four, these birds are now under your control. EVAC bodies to Tartarus Black Site and destroy. Stand by for future orders. Everyone else round-up and EXFIL to Amsterdam Airport."

After quickly promising to wire a six-figure donation and repair funds to Peter, we agreed to see each other in July for our annual motorcycle ride across Europe, and said our goodbyes. After I loaded six cases of his new Special Reserve Ale in a HELO, we hit the friendly skies without my Rosie.

I quickly realized Grace's stomach was as motion-sensitive as her mothers, thankfully, I got a bin bag to her in time. What worried me was that she didn't speak a single word. She just wrapped herself in her arms and gazed out the window crying. Silent tears ran down her wee, blue framed face, and then fell asleep. I wanted to console her, but didn't want to put her off. She had no idea who I was or how I am associated with her mam. *How will I find Rosie now?*

# Chapter Fourteen

After I ordered room service for myself and Grace, I sent everyone out of the Suite. Rosie was right, the girl was shy, as I observed she appeared overwhelmed with so many men in the Suite. After I contemplated the best way to approach the conversation. I sat down in the armchair opposite the sofa she curled upon.

I turned to Grace and said calmly said, "Gracie, I understand this is hard, but it is very important that we go over everything from the moment of your kidnapping, to the moment I took off your cuffs. I assume you don't want to think about this, but we need to bring your mam back and this is the only way." Grace was quiet in thought for several moments, then asked,

"Could I order a bottle of pink Moscato, please?

*Bloody hell, a whole bottle?*

"I'm beginning to see the method to your Mam's madness," I said as I shook my head with a crooked smile. I picked up the room's phone then called the kitchen. Shortly after, the chilled bottle appeared with our meals. After we ate on the sofa, and she drank *two* full glasses of wine, she finally started to talk.

"Thank you, I'm much calmer now. Early Saturday morning, I parked my bike to my spot at my apartment. I had been out super late with friends the night before and was only coming home. I was barely off my bike and these two guys snatched me and pulled me into their black van. I screamed but I still had my helmet on, so I don't think yelling did any good at four in the morning. I mean, no one was about at that hour.

"Once I was in the van, they put zip ties on my wrists. They told me to be quiet, and if I did, they wouldn't hurt me. I was so scared, I sat on the floor and cried in my helmet. They drove me to some house and two of them walked me inside holding my elbows.

"One man took off my helmet, and the other said he would take the zip tie off my wrists if I listened to what he said. He led me over to the sofa and told me to sit down. I did. He sat on the coffee table in front of me said, I would be in my room until they were done with me. In case I tried to leave, he would hurt my mom.

He said if I needed anything, just knock on my door, I had to tell one of the guards. I said OK, and he cut my zip ties off, then he strapped some box thing on my ankle. I think it was one of those house arrest ones they use on criminals back in the States.

"I guess they had taken my cell phone out of my jacket pocket because it was gone by the time I got to the room. There were no computers or tablets and the only phones I saw were the guards' cell phones, which they kept in their trouser pockets. They wore suits, so it's not as if I could bump into one and lift it. That's more Opals' thing anyway. She's excellent at getting her five-finger discount. She makes my mom and Lilly so mad with that. She's gonna get caught, you know."

I laughed to myself at the stark contrast between Grace and Opal, I steered her back to the house and asked, "What happened then at the house, Gracie? What was the house like?"

"The house was huge but there were alarms on all the doors and windows like my mom has at home. I had a huge room upstairs with only glass block windows, bathroom, and TV, so I stayed up on the bed and watched TV most of the time. A gigantic guard was outside my door too, because I could hear him talking off and on. They brought me food on trays, so I stayed on my bed."

I studied her the whole time she was speaking, and she was telling the truth. "Did they tell you what they wanted and how long you would be there?" She poured herself another glass of wine before she responded.

"No, only that it wouldn't be too long. One of the guards brought me a sandwich with tomatoes and lettuce, which I picked off, *so gross*. I must've fallen asleep during Dracula, because sometime that night, my bedroom door opened and my mom came in. She held me and we cried a lot. She had one of those boxes on her ankle too."

"Was your mam alright? Were there any marks on her?" I questioned with worry.

"She had some scratches on her hands, and her nails had broken which made her glitter gel polish peel. Opal says everything is better with glitter, and why mom wears it. She did say she tried to fight the men that took her. She had glass and bloody stuff in her hair, but she said it wasn't hers. She had an enormous knot on her head and bruises around her throat and on her arms. I think they did more to her than she told me. She said it was no big deal.

"They only wanted my Grandpa's painting, and they should release us soon, because they have it now. She asked if anyone had hurt me and I said other than the zip ties no. They didn't actually hurt either of us, other than her bruises."

I mulled over what Grace said as she surprised me and asking, "How do you know my mom, is she paying your company to help us?"

"I go into the cafe a lot, and she takes self-defense courses at my Security Company. We even talked about you and your sisters taking courses this summer." I told her. I didn't want to scare her, but she needed to understand her mam was in danger.

"Gracie, someone broke into your Mam's house Friday night and tried to steal the painting. Your Mam got into the safe room alright, though. My team and I came right away when she called. When I got to the bedroom and opened the false wall, my Rosie came right out of the room, just fine," I said smiling.

Grace nodded her head then paused in thought, lifted her palm to me and said,

"Wait, hold up. You called my mom, My Rosie. Nobody calls her Rosie. She hates it. It reminds her of those kids in that dark nursery rhyme that died. Are you dating my

mom?" She wondered aloud with an approving smile.


"We're getting to know each other, we haven't talked

about anything else," I said as I cleared my throat. My

nephews never asked me such awkward things. Suddenly her

eyes got huge and she said,


"OH-MY-GOD! Are you having S-E-X with my

mom?"


"No, I am not having S-E-X with your mam. Awe

Christ, now I'm spellin it. Nobody should talk about their

mother that way. That's just weird. I like her, I *really* like her

and I want to bring her back here, so I can take her out to

dinner, but I need to know where in the bloody hell she is." I

begged with my palms up in frustration. She nodded in

contemplation and redirected asking,

"How's Pete, is he OK? Did she bring him in the safe room, too?"

"Your mom took Pete to the vet, so you' need to ask her."

"What happened to Pete? Why'd he need to go to the vet?" She inquired as she looked up at me with big blue sad eyes and her bottom lip began to tremble.

"She'll tell you, lass."

"Pete's gone isn't he?" She whispered hanging her head. What could I say? I walked away from the chair and paced around the room. I tried to surmise what to confess. Finally, I decided the truth would be best. I looked down at her and said, "I'm sorry, but he's gone, pet." I confirmed as I nodded my head in defeat.

Grace hung her head and cried. I walked over and placed my hand out on hers on the sofa, but she pulled away and wrapped her arms around her middle. I couldn't bear the sight of the wee one as she cried. Is this how a parent feels? I felt this way when my nephews cried. It tore me up inside. After a few minutes, she regained her composure and poured the last of the wine in her glass. Sitting up she lifted her chin, wiped off her tears she asked,

"Can I order chocolate cake, please?"

I couldn't refuse her. I wanted the wee ones tears to stop. I couldn't bear her crying. Are all of Rosie's girls this sensitive? If they are, I want to take all of her girls under my wing and protect them from the world, especially anything that might involve crying. They shouldn't feel the need to shed a sorrowful tear ever again. It tears at my heart what they endured together. I picked up the phone and called the kitchen with her order. Anything I could do to comfort her would be a blessing. Only after I ordered did she continue.

"Thank you. Now, what other information can I give you so my mom can come home?"

"Grace, I am so sorry about Pete. I wanted to wait for your mam," I said shaking my head with remorse. I thought about her inquiry and continued.

"It's important we talk about the house. Was there a big garden, a pond, fence, anything? Did you see the outside of the house or the neighbor's house? What news shows did you watch on the TV, was it in English?" I inquired.

"The wall TV was in Dutch, the same as at my apartment, so I put the closed captioning in English like I normally would. We were on the coast, right on the water.

The pier I saw from the block window was a lot different from the one at our Lough House in Carlingford. It was really long and made of lumber like my grandparents have in Florida. I saw Muiderslot Castle way far off in the distance," she concluded.

"Praise Jesus, Alleluia! Let's bring up the images online, and we can figure out which house you were in. Do you want more wine?" I inquired, but she shook her head. Good, because I would have had to order another bottle to keep her talking.

As I booted up my laptop, I said "Gracie, can I ask you a personal question?"

"As long as it isn't *too* personal," she said hesitantly, looking down at her hands.

"Why do you and your mam spell your swear words?" At his, she broke out in a huge laugh, her eyes lit up at me, and her dimples showed, just like her mothers.

"If you swear around my Grandma, you have to spell it so it doesn't count. Then you won't dirty your soul. I think I do it out of habit anymore. I rarely swear, so it isn't a problem for me, but Opal swears like the Irish girls in school do. My mom babysits Kylie's little girl when Kylie's in class at Queens, so she probably keeps doing it since she can't spell yet."

I just sat back and smiled. Of course, it makes complete sense.

We scanned the satellite maps of the Amsterdam area coastline for nearly an hour. Grace found the house she and Rosie had been in. I sent a text with the coordinates to Sheelagh, instructing her to send Team One and Poseidon over in a HELO, and have two more Rovers delivered to the airport for them. Furthermore, secure two large RHIBs (Rigid Hull Inflatable Boat) from local salvage companies, and have the Crius Satellite view on infrared real-time to verify if Rose is actually still in the home.

"Did your mom say anything else about the men who took her, Grace? What they told her or anything else?"

"She said they told her she was a stupid woman in German. Mom knows some German from school, and from visiting Opal in Germany, I guess. They said they didn't want to take her, but she wouldn't stop fighting them. They had to grab the painting, so they didn't have a choice. I would assume they would be killed for not bringing it back to their boss. She said her man, Liam and his men were going to come look for us. She said he was helping her get me back in exchange for the painting. I guess that would be you."

"She said I was her man," I confirmed smiling and nodding.

"She said *her* man. In Northern Ireland, they refer to your man as, someone who is working with you or helping you. Like an expert." she advised. "Like, *your* man fixed my car," she added.

A knock at the door announced Gracie's chocolate cake had arrived. I answered the door as I thought to myself, *I am her man, whether she admits to it or not.* Gracie continued while she ate her cake.

"When we were in the room, she asked me about the guards and their cell phones. She kept checking the tides and marked them down on a napkin with the edge of the fork. They didn't give us a knife or a pen and paper. She said we could jump in, and swim to another pier down the coast if the tide was just beginning to go out. She said it would be cold, like our Lough, but at least we'll be away from them. We could have the guards to take us out on the pier at the right time and underwater swim. I'm not a good underwater swimmer, though. I didn't do that part well in my swimming lessons."

After her chocolate was eaten, I said, "Grace, one more thing, pet. How do you know Peter?" She smiled again, chuckled, and explained, "My Grandma and Grandpa like the Rectory's beer, but there is a daily limit. Maybe twice a year, in the summer, we'll drive to the Rectory on our way down to Paris. My Grandma and I buy our limit and take it to the car. When we're done loading it, we change clothes and put on hats. Then we walk back in and buy our limit again. Every summer we do this and every year, Father Peter busts me.

"Did you know, Grandma had me go in when I was only sixteen and buy booze for her? Talk about leading your grandkids the wrong way. I don't even like it. I've had one sip and that was enough." We had a good laugh as I stood, and ushered Grace to the bedroom saying,

"Come on, Grace, I'll show you your mom's room." I walked her to Rosie's room and turned on the light. I entered the bathroom, turned on the light, showing her the jet tub, she jumped for joy in surprise. I never knew such a simple thing could make every woman in the world happy. Hopefully, the blood is all cleaned up. After a quick scan of the tub and surrounding area, I handed her the bath salts saying,

"I'll see you in the morning. I'm going down to my men's Suite for now, but you have a guard at the door if you need anything. If I have to leave to bring your mam home before morning, I'll make sure you have two very nice bodyguards with you. They are on their way here now. Their names are Callum and Ian and will buy you anything you want from the shop downstairs. I'm not going to ask you to stay inside, but it might be best until I come back with your mam.

Don't go anywhere without Callum or Ian with you at all times.

"Order whatever you like from room service, and your mam like to sit on the balcony." I pointed to the bedside locker, saying, "Your mam's tablet and new mobile are here if you want. I'll buy you a replacement phone when we return home. Please keep all of this on the down-low until your mam's back. Her clothes are in the chest of drawers. Anything else ye need?" I asked.

"No, I'm fine. Liam, thank you for helping my mom and saving me. It was nice to see Father Peter again too."

"No worries, and Gracie, I didn't save you. You saved yourself *and* your mom by following their instruction. Goodnight," I said as backed out of the room closing the door.

I left the Suite, instructing Kian to guard Grace. I walked down to Bravo's Suite, and we began to strategize.

Riley cast the aerial view of the waterfront home on the TV. I informed my men that Team One and Poseidon were already in route. Riley pointed out the problem with the RHIB's coming in through the Amstel. They'd only be allowed to drive at wake speed, and it would take an extra hour before they were in place. We'd leave the Rovers back one klick out from the home. Delta will do Recon tonight while Zeus manned the drones.

There was a lot of activity in the home from the Crius Satellite feed at 0400 hours, so they could move at any moment. Most likely, they're scurrying about as Helmsmeier hadn't returned, and the German Mob at their backs. The German Mob is Italian and you don't want to cross paths with them. They shoot first and ask questions later, *if* you're still alive.

I quickly grabbed my mobile and rang Sheelagh, I ordered her to take down the hit on Helmsmeier. Also, as ordered she added a trail leading information that Helmsmeier moved back to his Base of Operations in Germany. Hopefully, that would turn the German's off of the home where Rosie was being held.

At 0500 hours, I received real-time confirmation, Rosie was still in the house. Poseidon, a team comprised of my best swimmers arrived with Callum and Ian. After receiving the Mission Brief, they will collect the RHIB's and proceed out on the open water to complete their orders.

I moved the Mission Briefing to one of Team B's main Suite, to ensure Gracie did not overhear me and become upset. I stood in front of my 21 men and began the Briefing:

"Mission Goal: Rescue Rose Kelly

"At 0400 hours to present, Crius Satellite feed confirmed Principal is in the home. Zeus One has eyes on the compound and verified she has not been moved. Heavy activity in the home confirms the guards ready to move or abandon the asset soon. Helmsmeier said, she'll blow at 1200 hours. Be on the lookout for EOD, trip wires, etc. Following Briefing, Poseidon will collect RHIB's and move to the position."

"Stage One: At 0700 hours, Zeus One maintains eyes on the compound from 300 meters up.

"Zeus Two: will keep eyes on the front windows at 200 meters out.

"Poseidon One, and Poseidon Two: will drive RHIB's and position one klick out from the compound at four and eight o'clock.

"Poseidon Three, and Poseidon Four: will underwater swim to the boathouse and disable the two known vessels, then return to the RHIB's.

"Stage Two: Delta and Bravo: will cut the electric to the compound and secure the perimeter silently. Two men on each side.

"Stage Three: Hotel and Cronus: will breach the house and secure Guards with any means necessary and Rescue Principal. Once Principal is obtained, confirm radio communication and all Teams EXFIL to Base II.

"Any questions?"

After I answered their questions, I finally said, "Callum and Ian, hang back after Briefing. Men, this may not be our biggest operation to date, but the most important to Cronus. If I have my way, Rose will be around permanently.

Poseidon's head out in immediately. Everyone else, Suit up, we head out at 0600 hours. Who Dares Wins, boys!" After hoots and hollers, the men headed out to complete their orders.

With just Callum and Ian in the room, I ordered "Under no circumstances is anyone allowed to yell at Gracie. Rosie and her girls are sensitive about yelling. They've had a rough past. Do not upset her, she's under enough stress with her mam gone and their dog dead. Tis one thing to yell or shout in an emergency, but another to yell because you can't control yourself. Give her whatever she wants. Buy her whatever she wants downstairs, but I swear, if you make her cry I'll break your arms and legs and bury you alive. I already made the wee one cry once, and I felt so bad it nearly broke my heart. So you understand, do not yell period."

"Yes, Sir," they said in unison.

# Chapter Fifteen
Rose

When I awakened up from our nap, yesterday, Gracie was gone. I don't remember when I fell asleep. Eating lunch with Gracie was the last thing I remembered. *Did they drug my food?*

Eavesdropping, I overheard the guards talking outside my door. My German needed to be a little dusted off, but I retained enough to understand them. They took her to Cronus, whoever that was. Over my dead body if I'd leave my daughter to another mad man. Is he with the Greek Mob? Cronus was a powerful god from Greek Mythology, and I don't like the sound of him. I need to reach Liam, then we need to find out who Cronus is and bring Gracie back. If anyone could, it would be him.

I will find a way out of here to the water and call Liam, then find my daughter. With all of his resources, if anyone would find her he would. Sheelagh surprised me with all the information she found out about the painting. It had been hanging in our house my whole life, and the whole time my Grandfather deceived us all. Why? Although she angered me, she is great at her job. She knows what she's doing. No wonder Liam hired her.

I was not as good a swimmer as my Mom, but I'm not half bad. In early May and the water will be cold, but it won't be deadly.

With it being dusk, I examined the water, through the glass block window, I studied the waves again. Nearly a day later, I figured out the tide table. I marked it on my log like I had this morning. Taking a run for it as the tide was rolling out, I would shoot straight out, from the pier, and swim fifty yards out. I would catch the current running south toward City Center. When the tide was rolling in, I was screwed.

I sat down at the small table in the room and searched for anything that might be helpful to use as a weapon. The room was huge. It was as big as the Suite at our hotel. The bedposts were bolted into the bed rails, and I couldn't budge the nuts. There were no curtains, only vertical blinds with no wand for shifting them open or closed.

They checked my silverware every time they took the tray back and only gave me unbreakable plastic cups and plates. The dresser and nightstand drawers didn't pull all the way out. I would break one down and hit someone with it. No bedside lamps or cords of any kind were about. The TV also had a short plug that went directly into the eye height socket behind the TV on the wall.

I knelt and laid on the floor like a child, looking at the room from a different perspective. Maybe then, I would find something I could use as a weapon. Laying down for the longest time I came up with nothing. Getting up off the floor and moved to the bathroom. Maybe I would find something in there.

I walked into the bathroom and sat on the floor. I checked all the cabinets, but found nothing. Just soaps and a small bag of bath salts. Not a shower curtain, cleaning supplies, or towel bar to be found. The towels were folded in a stack on the vanity.

Thankfully, the bathroom had a huge bathtub. Not a jet tub, though. I thought to add the rose-scented bath salts to my bath, but quickly decided against it. Why would I want to smell like someone else's Grandmother? Trying to relax, I filled the tub with hot water and tried to relax. I didn't care if it hurt the house arrest box on my ankle. *Screw them.*

I thought back to when the man on the motorbike stopped. He told me I had sixty seconds to run to the far west end of the Moco to exchange the painting for my daughter. Had he known I brought Liam and the Beards? Did he tell me to run, because he knew Liam wouldn't be as fast? Any of the Beards would run after me. Liam can run, he ran after me shouting. I couldn't stop and risk Gracie's life by slowing down for two sentences, or Helmsmeier would become aware I brought support. I made the wrong choices, though. In hindsight, if I slowed down for him to catch up he would provide support for the exchange.

Did they see the snipers in their hides? No, the Beards know what they were doing. They stayed alive all these years, they wouldn't make a foolish mistake and be seen. Like Liam ordered, they would use their shields. Those must be some form of camouflage cover. Perhaps, he was aware of Liam's involvement already.

Maybe they observed us from higher up somewhere else? I guess not. There were no other tall buildings in the area. They had to have planned the change in meeting place all along and moved the meeting point to ensure a gap in my protection. That had to be it.

They didn't even bring Gracie. Why didn't they bring her? What would I do, if I was a criminal? I would make sure to secure the painting first. I wouldn't risk losing their hostage. Is that what they wanted all along? They would release Gracie eventually, I pray. Because they haven't harmed either of us in any way up until they gave Grace to Cronus. I pray Cronus or the German Mob aren't traffickers'. No, we were treated too well. Traffickers would put us in cages, or, so I read.

I think they would let us both go, in a short time. They're planning on leaving me to Cronus or the German Mob anyway. The next question is, when I can run away. I need to connect with Liam, and we can find Cronus.

Realizing, I had only frustrated myself in the bathtub worrying about the past and not the present I was done. Stepping out of the bathtub I dried myself off and redressed, sans panties, and bra. Second-day underwear is not my bag. I washed those in the sink, towel drying them, then hung them on the radiator.

I began my grounding exercises to stop my mind from running while trying to go to sleep. I missed Liam and Gracie something awful. I worried what Gracie was going through with Cronus, and begged God to keep her safe in His arms. Liam must be beside himself with us both gone. This whole thing went sideways because I ran. I did that. This is my fault.

How in the world will Liam find us? Having grown so addicted to him, I can't think straight. Addicted? Is that the right word? No. Fallen is the right word. *I have fallen for him. Completely.*

I recited my Divine Mercy Rosary, as usual, and tried

to drift off to sleep in exhaustion, but my mind wouldn't let

me. What is Gracie doing now? Please, Lord, keep her safe.

Don't let anyone hurt her. I beg you to shield her in the arms

of The Holy Spirit. I understand that I'm not a good person. I

curse at people while driving. I don't go to mass like I should

and I'm sorry. I'm sorry for all of it. I'm sorry I tormented my

sisters and brother, and stole that belt in the third grade.

Please, God, forgive me and keep Gracie out of harm's way.


#


The next morning I woke to the sunrise. I laid in bed

sometime before I redressed in my undergarments. I walked to

the glass block window and watched the tide. High tide, but it

hadn't started to recede as yet. Today *has* to be the day I do this. I can't wait for another. I won't. Now, how the hell do I get out of this bedroom?

My personal ape carried my breakfast tray to my small table, as usual. The man looked like he was part orangutan. All he needed was to drag his knuckles and the appearance would be complete. An orangutan in a suit. Wouldn't you like to spy that at the zoo?

I consumed my breakfast of instant coffee, boxed juice, and stale Danish pastries with contempt. If Liam were here, we would laugh and share this awful breakfast. Of course, he'd have his shirt off and wear an old pair of 501's, with the top button undone.

Looking out the window again I spied a storm as it rolled in from the northwest. With the gloom of the impending weather, I wonder if this would truly be the best time to run, but how? How can I get out of this room? How badly would the storm impede my swimming? With its direction, it would most likely aid it. I don't think that old wives' tale to wait an hour after you eat was true. Finishing my coffee I set my cup down as the power went out.

Everything was quiet, I could lightly hear the wind that was kicking up with the storm. It wouldn't have hit the city center yet, so I doubt it was that unless it took out a transformer by the house here. The wind started to howl. I looked down at my tray, but I didn't have any silverware this morning. Taking all the dishes off of the tray and tossed it on the end of the bed, and waited.

Then I heard it. Gunfire rang out downstairs and men were yelling, in the hallway outside my room. My blood pressure rose as I suddenly stood in question; how in the hell I would reach the pier now with *two* groups of killers in the house.

My door abruptly flew open and Gigantor, the biggest ape bodyguard, slammed my door shut. He stalked toward me from across the big room as he waved his arms at me shouting,

"We have to go! They are attacking us!" Still shouting, he pulled out a ring of keys and unlocked the other door in the room. This room had a balcony as I quickly ran to it and opened the glass door wall.

"I'm not going anywhere with you," I shouted back.

"We have to go, they will kill us all! Helmsmeier owes the Mob the statue. He needed the painting to find the statue, and they promised to kill everyone unless he handed it over this morning!" He bellowed as he snatched my arm and tried to drag me over the balcony. That was certain death. Pulling myself from his grasp, I attempted to get into position.

"I-WILL-NOT-GO-WITH-YOU!" With my hands in fists, I screamed kicking my feet and scratched like a rabid feline. Finally, I kicked myself free. I rolled to my knees, and stood, as he laughed at me. My hands in fists at my sides and my chin up in defiance.

Lightning lit up the storm darkened room, followed by a huge boom of thunder. A colossal rainfall started with the wind blowing into the room at an awe-inspiring speed. Sheets of rain began whipping into the room through the open glass door wall as they pelted us. Being from tornado alley, if I didn't know better, I'd say a tornado coming. When large hail begins to bounce down, and the wind howls like a steam engine, we'll all be screwed.

"You have to come with me! Helmsmeier will kill me if I leave without you!" He yelled at me through the storm. Rain showered his face. He lunged toward me again. At the last moment, I reached for the bedpost as he captured my other arm, attempting to drag me to him again. He failed and I dropped to the ground. In my peripheral vision, I saw him coming for me again, and I clung with all my strength to the bottom of the bedpost. Snatching both of my feet, he jerked my body so hard, it decompressed my spine. After the initial shock of pain subsided, I gave one final kick and lost my gym shoe. The ape fell to the ground on his backside.

Scrambling to the open glass door wall to the balcony, I turned around and screamed. "Leave without me, or they'll kill you downstairs! I don't care! I'm not leaving," I screamed as I stood. The wind was whipping my hair in my face, and my backside getting drenched from the incoming rainstorm. I pointed outside over the lawn, "Look! Look out this balcony and tell me what you see! They've surrounded us!"

As the ape stalked over to the glass door wall, passing me, and stepped outside on the balcony, he peered over the short iron railing to view the commotion of men in camouflage below. I slowly crept back out of his way and kept my pace until my back hit the door of the huge bedroom. This was my chance. I bent over and silently charged him like a raged bull. I hit him with my shoulder right in the upper back to throw him forward off balance. He flew over the short balcony with me attached to his back. Time stopped as I wondered if I was too stupid to live, or if this is the smartest thing I had ever done.

We landed with a thud that knocked the wind out of me, with me on his back, as I heard his head smash the side of the seawall making a hollow sound like a watermelon. Attempting to take the biggest breath I was doing my level best to stand. I noticed blood mixed with fresh rain and seawater as it showered the seawall pooling beneath his head. *Whatever.* He made his choices.

Purposefully not looking around me and with one shoe, I took off in a fast sprint down the pier. I thought I had heard multiple men shouting, but I wasn't about to turn

around, as I dove into the water at an angle just as planned.

Ankle box be damned, I was out and was not coming back.

# Part Three

# Chapter Sixteen
Liam

At 0800 hours, with Zeus and Poseidon in position, I received confirmation the boathouse vessels had been disabled. "Delta, go." "Bravo, go." I held back and awaited confirmation the perimeter was secure. Delta and Bravo breached the compound. After they secured the perimeter, they took out three tangos silently.

"Hotel, go." Hotel cut the electric, and soundlessly we walked to our predetermined entry points. Giving my hand signal for go, and we simultaneously breached the house.

The wind was whipping about as a colossal thunderstorm started, as Zeus One confirmed at least ten more guards were inside between the ground and first floors. The last sighting confirmed Rosie sitting upstairs. I wasn't about to call her out with unknowns in the house, as she needs to stay out of the line of fire. I'll get to her soon enough.

After I shot the guard closest to the front door, in the back of his head, I was charged by an unknown from behind and catapulted forward down the few foyer stairs. Landing on my stomach and quickly flipped my body around, effectively dismounting him from my back, but, unfortunately, I dropped my weapon in the process. He was unarmed, or he would have shot me instead of jumped me.

As I reached for my weapon, he jumped on top of my abdomen and punched me in my left eye socket several times. Each time he connected with my skin, I slightly pushed myself with my feet toward my weapon. Quickly arching my back to throw off his balance I shifted the attacker off of myself enough that I reached for my SIG, raised my weapon, and shot him in the throat. He fell next to me, with a rapidly growing pool of blood. "Four down," I relayed in my com.

Wobbling as I tried to stand up I realized the fall had fucked up my prosthetic. After standing, I noticed the joint rivet had popped between my outer sleeve and calf. I stumbled like a drunk. *This is why I don't do wet work anymore.*

After I verified we had secured the first floor I moved to the stairs. I did my best thanks to the adrenaline running through my system, and made my way up the stairs with my jacked lower limb. "Cronus, breaching the first floor now, over," I relayed to my teams.

Using the wall in front of me for stability while continuing to use my right leg as primary, I peered around the corner down the hall to the bedrooms. Two shots rang out as I quickly retreated to my original position. My left arm stung and I glanced down to see if it kissed or a bit me. Looking down at my arm, through the burned and torn fabric, I confirmed it definitely bit me. No exit wound. My nostrils filled with the smell of burnt flesh and copper. Thank God I'm a dead shot with either hand.

Steadying my breathing, I drew my SIG and stabilized my stance as I turned around the corner. In those few moments, he had already moved 10 meters closer. I double-tapped him between the eyes, he dropped like a rag doll. "Five down," I relayed in my com as I continued to clear the rooms off the hallway, on my way to Rosie.

"Cronus, tango, room one, west side, over." Zeus Two instructed in my com. I clicked once, confirming receipt of transmission. The first room to the left was small like an office. Hugging the wall, I reached over and opened the door, shielding myself from the side, and waited. Not a sound. Entering cautiously with my weapon up, I turned right double-tapping the thug between the eyes. "Six down," I relayed. I finished clearing the room and continued.

"Cronus, two individuals engaged, room three west," Zeus Two advised. With one click, I verified receipt of transmission. I heard yelling from one of the rooms. As I hobbled my way there, I recognized Rosie's bloodcurdling scream as my hobble became a run. As I opened it, Rosie jumped through the window with a guard at her front. "No!" I screamed and tottered through the glass door wall and peered down over the balcony. She must have landed on top of the guard in the garden because, she was already up and took off at a fast clip down the pier as I yelled, "Rosie stop!" She didn't turn around, instead she dove off the pier and was gone from sight. *Sweet Jesus, why Rosie, why?*

Why does that woman do the opposite of what I want every damn time? Why does she test me this way? Hobbling downstairs the best I could, I limped down the pier. Simon was already there and wanted to dive in, but I ordered him to stand down. He kept yelling out to her in the hope she'd bloody listen for once. While I threw off my prosthetic and sleeve, tactical vests and belt, and boots. I hit my com and commanded, "Bravo One in command, over!" I awaited Riley's confirmation click, then attempted to dive in to find her. I could still swim missing half my leg from the calf down. Just not as well.

Diving in, I swam straight out, just like Rosie had. I hoped Grace was right, she would swim out to the current, then down to another house. Hopefully, Simon would clue my men in on what just transpired. I swam with a breaststroke technique. I could only do so much with one leg to kick. She was too far ahead of me. I stopped when I saw her surface in the current. I called out to her, "Rosie stop!" She stopped, turning around and looked my way.

Beginning my freestyle, once I hit the current, ten meters in front of me, I continued to look for her, but she was gone. Swimming in place for a moment, I waited for her to surface for her next breath, but she never came back up. Something was wrong, and I felt my skin crawl with invisible spiders. I continued my freestyle to where I had seen her last, but she was gone. With my mobile on the pier and com underwater, I was useless. Waving to Joe, who was right behind me, he stopped. I lifted my body into the hull. I don't understand. Something isn't right, she's a strong swimmer.

# Chapter Seventeen
Rose

Diving into the water at a forty-five-degree angle, thankfully, I didn't hit bottom. I swam as fast as my body would go, straight out underwater as far as I dare without taking a breath. I resurfaced to breathe, and dove underwater again, to swim as far as I could. Suddenly, the current caught me and took me South as I predicted. The shock of the cold North Sea stung worse than The Irish Sea in July, but I had to keep on. I needed to swim far enough away from the pier without anyone seeing me as they wouldn't be able to shoot me that far out. I plunged under the surface again and continued my underwater swim.

Catching the current, I double-timed it south. I can swim another twenty houses down, I would reach a pier and call Liam and the Dutch Police for help. Without much sleep and an unhealthy breakfast, I was exhausted.

Swimming along with the current as far down as I was able, my mouth tasted like foul saltwater. My body warmed up the longer I was in motion, but the pressure on my chest was overwhelming. I realized my hearing aid, was gone, but it was replaceable. What's another ten grand? I couldn't let my girls down and allow myself to succumb to those criminals and I won't leave Gracie in the hands of Cronus. Even if I froze or drowned out here, though, I would have gone down fighting.

Kicking my legs and came up to breathe as I counted the houses. Ten. Keep on going Sugar, you've almost made it, my Grandpa cheered me on internally. I captured a deep breath and kept going. Using my bare left foot, I kicked off my right shoe as it caused drag. Resurfacing only to breathe I kept going. Breaching the surface again, I counted the houses.

Five more and I should be fine. The houses were so far apart with their magnificent green lawns. It felt like I had been swimming for ages.

If I reached that channel entrance, where there're apartments, no one would see where I exited the water. I breathed, ready to swim down again, briefly I thought Liam called my name and I stopped. *Did I just hear that or am I dead?* Looking around behind me, I peered in the distance for some time. Eventually, I spied someone's arms swimming toward me far back from the Germans pier. Before I called out to him, someone grabbed my legs from below the surface and jerked me under the surface.

I kicked at the person again and again, but they wouldn't release me. The person scaled up my body and snatched a hold of my torso. Was he going to drag me down farther underwater? Finally, after kicking myself up and pushing his arms off of me for an eternity, I breached the surface. In full scuba gear, a man appeared the surface, but wouldn't let me go no matter how hard I kicked. He reached up and took off his re breather, he spoke, then winced in pain.

"Do not make a sound or you die," he said in a menacing tone. I froze. He put an independent air hose, from his second tank to my mouth, and dragged me underwater again. He underwater swam quite a ways out from the channel, as the pressure on my chest was near overwhelming. Thank God I had gone scuba diving in Mexico and I had already known how to use the re breather. We continued to underwater swim at about six feet in depth for what seemed like forever.

My skin reverberated with the familiar buzz of a boat motor and I opened my eyes before I ran into its stern anchor line and hull. Thank God the boat was idle. Swimming into a prop is not on my to-do list. When we resurfaced, I realized we had reached a small yacht. Scuba thug led me to the swim platform, and flipped down the ladder from the swim platform saying, "Go up, now."

I looked around, but the boat was blocking my view of the shore. Slowly, I did as I was told as my frozen fingers tightened on the first rung. I tried to lift my right leg higher, knowing the ladder was inches away, but I couldn't quite lift my stiff knee joint up far enough, in my tight wet jeans. Finally, after swearing at me, in God knows what language, he lifted my foot to the last rung. He pushed my bulbous butt up to where I was standing. I was so heavy in my wet clothes. After three more rungs, I finally made it on to the swim platform.

Four goons were waiting for me on the other side of the platform, and they looked *deadly*. Are these Cronus' men? No, they couldn't be. These men must be the German Mob, not Greek. They all had an olive complexion, though, and wore black tactical clothing and a sidearm. Their sculpted muscles protruded from their long-sleeve tees, like Liam and his men. Putting their big meaty hands under my frozen arms, they dragged me over the stern of the boat to the cabin. They forcefully threw me down the cabin steps to the floor screaming at me.

Shaking from the cold, my body was too stiff to have gone fetal. My hands were fisting and I'm sure my lips were blue. I had seen a blanket on the side of the v-berth, with one pillow before they pushed me. All I wanted to do was sleep. I was in the water for too long, and I knew it. My vision blurred and my vertigo was in full swing as the waves continued crashing into the boat. My body still held the simulation of floating in the water, and I was dazed.

I couldn't make out what he was saying with his accent, as I could hear him, but not understand him. The thug kept screaming at me, as if that would help me understand him. Far away, I heard the clanking of the electric bow anchor being lifted, then the boat started moving. The white red

interior lights automatically switched to red that permeated the

cabin in an eerie glow.

Two men walked down the steps and stood above me,

flailing their arms around yelling at one another, yet I couldn't

understand what language they were speaking in. Both men

turned to watched me as I moved my icy-cold arm slowly and

lifted my right hand to my ear. I gradually lifted my left hand

and placed it flat in front of my chest. Moving my hand from

my ear to my lower hand, I signed I am deaf. I signed it over

and over, but he didn't understand. I think I had it right, but I

was too exhausted to care. Opal had shown me a few things in

her British Sign Language Course she took at the local college

last year.

Finally, with the last of my energy, I mimicked writing

on my open palm. Eventually, after repeating it several times,

they looked around in the cabin drawers and handed me paper

and a pen. Writing, I-AM-DEAF, I turned the paper facing

them. The pen and paper slipped from my icy hands the floor.

The screamer took the paper from me and laughed.

They all started to laugh and spoke in something that sounded

like Spanish, but not quite, but it certainly wasn't Greek.

Maybe they're speaking Italian. Italian sounds a lot like

Spanish. The diver came inside and told the men something

curious, from my best attempt at translation, he had to obtain

the statue and a hostage, swimming them back to the boat.

The entire cabin reeked in their cologne and chemicals

from the new carpet and fiberglass interior as they continued

arguing with each other. I think they argued about transferring

me off of the floor, because the one man kept pointing at me

with his arm and hand at me. Two men bent down and lifted

me by my armpits and not so gently shoved me on to the v-

berth. I un-fisted my icy fingers snatching the pillow and

blanket, poorly attempting to wrap myself. I snuggled onto the pillow and turned into myself, curling my knees-up to my chest.

Shaking like a leaf, the man who gave me the paper, pulled out his cell phone and showed me a picture of a metal sculpture. Shaking my head, I closed my eyes quickly, hoping he had not read my eyes. He collected the paper and pen off the floor and pushed it to me. I wrote: NO SCULPTURE, on the paper, but I kept my head down and did not look at him. He continued to yell at me for the longest time. I finally wrote: HE KIDNAPPED ME FOR PAINTING. NO SCULPTURE. The men yelled at me, then amongst themselves.

Bone-weary, I closed my eyes, against my better judgment, and woke up when I was violently smacked across the face. He shoved the paper at me again and as I trembled, I wrote: I DID NOT SEE SCULPTURE. I HAVE NO SCULPTURE! I closed my eyes in exhaustion, after they turned to argue amongst themselves again.

Cautiously, I opened my eyes and peered around the cabin. I hadn't seen a fly-bridge from the ladder. Most likely it's a twin-engine inboard. I can pilot a twin-engine with my eyes closed. Being a smaller yacht and it had no interior helm, like our old yacht on Lake Erie. If it did, I could take over piloting the boat if I could just haul myself up.

I'd have to wait for my body to warm up some. At the rate my body shook, it would be some time before that happened. Pain consumed my body as muscles convulsed. The galley looked brand new and un-lived in. If I transferred myself to the kitchen drawers, possibly one would contain a blade. Even a fillet knife would do, although, I didn't see any fishing equipment.

The drawers under the kitchen table most likely held an independent boat horn. I could pound the bottom lip on one thug's head. I would imagine all boats, even outside the States would be required to carry one. Mentally, I indexed list of items legally required to keep on a boat this size in the States. Boating laws are mostly universal between Canada and the US. I'm not sure about Europe, though. Medical kit, life vests, boat cushion, life ring, boat horn, fire extinguisher, flare gun. FIRE EXTINGUISHER and FLARE GUN!

Continuing my perusal of the cabin's red interior while I tried to stretch out my fingers and legs. Any circulation would be good at this point, as I stretched my legs out as far as I dare on the v-berth, and did my best to wiggle my toes. Still exhausted I wanted to close my eyes so badly, but I knew that was a stage of hypothermia. No heat was in the cabin and even though the bulk of the storm was over, it was still quite dark outside. The wind was still whipping in from the open cabin door.

Moving my legs apart, I tried to make my hip joints mobile. Lifting my arms I attempted the same with my shoulders. The muscles in my neck, back, and abdomen were now wrought with spasms along with my shivers which was more painful than I thought it would be, but I've been through worse.

Two thugs reentered the cabin talking amongst themselves. The thug with the big gold chain necklace pulled his cell phone out of his pants pocket, and called someone on speaker. They both argued with the man on the phone, presumably their superior. Whatever their plans were, didn't pan out. According to the man's voice on the phone, they were up the creek without a paddle.

Under the blanket, I kept up as I flexed my fingers and toes to encourage circulation. After their barking dog fight on the phone, they ended the call. Walking back out on the rear deck, they closed the cabin door. Finally. I slowly swung my legs forward off the v-berth onto the floor. Lifting my right arm, I pushed my stiff body up to a sitting position. Staying there I studied my surroundings until I thought I could stand. There was no aft cabin, so I must start here.

Finally, making my move, my right hand gripped the back of the kitchen seat bench as support as I slowly stood. Bending over quietly, I pulled out the first drawer under the seat bench, rifling through the drawer, finding charts, and the boat's manuals. I silently closed the drawer. Taking two steps forward, still bent over, I noiselessly opened the drawer under the second seat bench. Voila! The boat's emergency kit was in a dry flotation bag.

As soundlessly as I could, I unzipped the top and rifled through the bag until I found the flare gun and three extra flares. I quietly flipped the bag top over and closed the drawer. Taking the flare gun, I pushed it in my waist at the back of my jeans and put the small flares in my back jean pocket.

Standing upright again and turned to the left. There were four utensil drawers under the built-in flat stainless steel dish strainer. Before I had a chance to open one, Thug Gold Chain stormed at me yelling as he stepped down into the cabin. He lifted his arm to punch me and my old knee-jerk reaction kicked in as I cowered and covered my face. The blow came fast, but not as bad as I expected. It knocked me onto the floor again, as I hit my head on the hard fiberglass edge of the v-berth on the way down.

Waking up, sometime later, still on the floor, I realized that we had stopped moving and I tried lifting my head and peered around. Ouch! My head hurt so badly. Looking at all of them as they all gathered around the kitchen table; talking amongst themselves about a gabbia and I don't know what. At least they weren't yelling any longer. Knowing my head couldn't take much more, I needed to get off of this smelly floor. Thankfully, I stopped shivering as badly as I was before, but they still didn't turn the heat on. We stopped moving in the open water.

Closing my eyes first, I listened to the water. There was a slight sway of the boat, followed by a clink. Then we floated back again the other way and I heard another light clink. We're tied off and probably docked at a marina. Deciding I should plan my use of the flare gun now. I would shoot the top of the table, then reload. Maybe, I would then shoot the cabin walkway to force them inside. Then, I would follow them out to the aft deck, as the carpet would catch fire. From there I will run and find another boater. It's May and people would be about, preparing for their summer boat trips.

Moving my arm around to my front I pushed myself into a sitting position, and slowly, I brought my stiff knees around underneath me and began to stand. I kept my back toward the v-berth, so they didn't see my flare gun and I held on to the galley counter to support myself as I wasn't entirely sure I was going to make it all the way up. If I didn't balance myself properly, I might fall on my throbbing face. Once I achingly stood, the thug with the gold chain was standing in-between me and the cabin door. He just stood there and stared at me, as if he could read my mind.

I backed myself up to the v-berth when a huge explosion happened on the far offshore. My head instinctively turned my head to the window. Quickly, I turned the other direction to verify where we were. We're at a Marina. With my right hand, I reached behind me and grasped the 12 gauge flare gun. Before I had a chance to pull my weapon, he stalked to me with a venomous sneer. Within two strides, he punched me in the face and everything went black.

# Chapter Eighteen
Liam

Poseidon One came alongside me and I lifted myself into the RHIB. "Where's she? Hand me your spare com," I demanded Joe (Poseidon One), as mine was in the drink. As the wind lashed and the rain hit my face painfully, I hit my new com and commanded, "Cronus: Poseidon One, Two, Three, Four, anchor and dive! Anchor and dive! Find Principal Scoot! She dove in from the pier and swam South with the current. I repeat, South current. Zeus, I want all drones scanning the water and recording. Any explosives confirmed, over?"

"Bravo One, Affirmative, two disarmed, with two more to go. Five hundred meter blast zone. I ran EVAC on the Compound five minutes ago. No time left, Boss. Over."

"Everyone confirmed, Bravo One, over?"

"Affirmative. Over."

"Delta, Hotel, Bravo, walk ten piers forward with eyes peeled if she left a trail, go!"

"I'll pilot the RHIB," I said and took over for Joe. "Where's your mobile?" I asked before he rolled back into the water. Picking up his mobile, I called Sheelagh. "What's wrong, Joe?" she inquired.

"Cronus," I answered her.

"What's wrong Sir," she asked.

"Scan all Zeus footage and Crius Satellite view from the point when Rosie jumped off the pier forward. She's somewhere in the water and something is wrong. I saw the way she dove in the water. She swam so fast, she knows what she's doing. She planned on underwater swimming down the waterfront and getting help. Grace said she's a strong underwater swimmer. It's a Blitzer with this wind and rain, but no way dinna she make it. She might be hidden, and doesn't realize that we're here.

"It is entirely possible the Mob took her if they were planning a water attack, but I don't see any other boats within two klicks of us. Call me on this phone. Mine's in the drink. Go." I ended the call and tapped my com, "Zeus One and Two, find anything, over."

"Negative, Zeus One, over."

"Negative, Zeus Two, over."

Staying put was the hardest thing I ever had to do, but I couldn't run over my men. Four divers scattered throughout the south current and I canna move. I can't believe I lost her again. I would have had her if she hadn't taken off.

Thankfully, there was a captain's bench as I stood up and hopped a few steps to pilot the wheel. Picking up Joe's spotter scope I scanned the surface for Rosie. The rain continued to pelt my skin as I hit my com again commanding,

"Delta One, Hotel One, and Bravo One, any signs, over?"

"Delta One, Negative, over."

"Hotel One, Negative, over."

"Bravo One, Negative, over."

Since she didn't reach the pier, she could have caught an underwater river, and been carried somewhere else. But where she went it, the water wouldn't be deep enough for that. It made no sense, I thought as the rain continued to batter me.

Poseidon Team dove the south current for the next hour as I checked in repeatedly with each team. I lost my woman twice. I don't deserve to have her, Lord. Poseidon was running out of air. The weather started to lighten, but it was still Baltic.

One hour and forty-two minutes into the rescue, Sheelagh rang. "Cronus," I answered.

"Sir, I viewed on satellite imagery, the principal was approximately fifteen houses down when she was greeted by a diver. Not one of ours sir. He underwater swam her to a small yacht by the park, two klicks down. They moved to the Marina by Almere Poort. I have sight of them at the marina, Sir."

"That's easily three klicks away, on the other side on Almere Poort."

"Aye, Sir."

"What's the name of the boat?"

"Sophia, Sir."

"Keep an eye on that Marina and tell me if anyone leaves port." I ended the call and rounded my men. Knowing Poseidon wouldn't have underwater com on this operation, they will be up soon enough when they ran out of air.

Just then the house exploded in a huge fireball. I had to duck down and cover myself. Bricks, roofing tiles, and other debris rained down in front of us. I hit my com and commanded, "Roll call!" Everyone chimed in one after the other except Poseidon,

"Bravo One"

"Bravo Two."

"Bravo Three."

"Cronus, who's got my leg, over?" I requested.

"Hotel Three, Sir," Simon confirmed.

"Delta, Bravo, Zeus, EXFIL to Marina at Almere Poort for recognizance. Principal spotted with diver at Marina in a small white yacht named Sophia. Stand by for future orders." All men responded.

"Hotel, meet Poseidon One at the beach, south of the Marina at Almere Poort for Rendezvous, over."

One by one, my Poseidon team members surfaced. After they were in their RHIB's with their com on they received their briefing. Lastly, Joe finally came back with Rosie's shoe. Pulling anchor we headed over to the beach on the other side of the river. The rain was lighter, but still vicious with the speed we traveled. We could barely see anything as the rain pelted our eyes with wind coming straight at us from the northwest. I'd been through worse, but only in Scotland.

"Poseidon Two, position a one klick outside the marina and prepare for possible Underway Ship Assault, over."

Joe ran the RHIB right up on the beach and Simon ran my leg out to me. He had removed the broken pin and replaced it with a makeshift nut and bolt. He always carried the weirdest stuff on him. After I attached it and jumped off, Simon and I shoved Joe off the beach back to the water. I followed Simon to the Rover, and we drove to the Marina.

Simon also found Rosie's other shoe inside the house. Her hearing aid box, Shelby, was outside next to the overgrown ape Rosie landed on top of. I instructed Hotel at the Rover, "Marina for recognizance, go!"

Hotel drove up to the other Rovers at Rendezvous. Sophia didn't move from the last slip number in the third finger pier, and drones show five individuals on board. One in the v-berth, four in galley. Sheelagh was working on identifying them, with her newest facial recognition software.

"Poseidon two and four, disable vessel below the surface, go."

Two clicks followed in response. Hopefully, they had enough air left in their tanks. If not, I knew they'd change their approach to cover themselves from view.

Once Poseidon confirmed the vessel was disabled, we'd begin our assault. I turned to my men and clicked my com for Briefing.

"Mission Goal: Rescue Rose Kelly

"With this much time in the water, Principal has most likely moderate hypothermia. She'll need EVAC to Amsterdam UMC. Hotel One, Two, and Cronus will EVAC with Primary to Hospital.

Stage one is in process. Poseidon two and four are currently disabling the vessel below the surface.

Stage Two: Delta, vessels on either side of Sophia are empty. Silently board and prepare for an assault from bow and stern, heavy on port and starboard close to the Sophia. Hold for go.

Stage Three: Hotel, secure perimeter in case of breach on pier surrounding the vessel, and create a disturbance with flashbangs. Hold for go.

Stage Four: Bravo, silently position onboard vessel prepare for all tangos to exit cabin and silence and secure principal. Use silent force as needed. Leave the bodies in the drink. Hold for go."

"Poseidon One and Three: As long as the principal is secure, no need to engage in Underway Ship Assault. Poseidon, only engage for Ship Assault if the principal is moved to another vessel. Hold for go."

All teams chimed in acceptance.

We all sat in wait for the confirmation from Poseidon. Approximately twenty minutes in, we received confirmation of vessel decommission, I began, "Delta position go, Bravo position go. Hotel position go." Like clockwork, my troopers got into position and relayed.

"Delta One, ready for go, over."

"Hotel One, ready for go, over."

"Bravo One, ready for go, over."

"Poseidon One, ready for go, over."

"Poseidon Three, ready for go, over."

Once I received confirmation of everyone was in place, I ordered, "Hotel go." Two flash bangs were set off in thirty-second succession, one hundred feet apart, and three tangos sprinted outside the cabin of the Sophia. Riley, Evan, and Kenneth all took down one man silently with their blades, dropping them noiselessly in the drink.

Riley held up one finger signaling one man remained inside the cabin. We all stood by awaiting the fourth. Nothing.

"Riley, softly breach cabin door, take out the fourth tango, go."

I watched as Riley slowly opened the cabin door and placed the head of his weapon inside. One suppressed shot and the tango was dead.

"Four down. Clearing cabin now, over." Riley chimed in. I ran down the pier silently praying Rosie was still alive. When I arrived, Kenneth was dropping the fourth tango in the drink. Riley was bent over the v-berth picking the lock on a cage. *They put my woman in a cage!*

Riley quickly picked the lock as I lifted the top. Riley lifted Rosie out of a cage built underneath v-berth on top of the fresh water tank. I followed him out as he turned to carry her off the boat. Carefully, I took her from him once he stepped off the boat. I carried her under her legs and behind her back, and hustled my woman down the pier, ordering in my com, "Simon and Charlie drive us to Hospital." They met us at the Rover, where I ordered Riley to take over my command. Over my com, I heard. "Bravo One in Command. Roll call."

"Bravo Two."

"Bravo Three."

I listened as I gently loaded my icy goddess in the Rover. Charlie held her from the other side of the vehicle as I climbed in. After lifting her on to my lap, Simon drove us off to Amsterdam UMC Hospital. I looked down at Rosie in my arms. Her poor body was frozen nearly solid with her muscles quivering. Her lips were blue and her skin was pale white.

Charlie, climbed over the seats to the back and pulled an emergency thermal blanket out of his go-bag. He shook it out and handed it to me, helping me cover her up. He also activated several warming packs and held them to her bare feet. Simon drove us to hospital at a fast clip. I kept trying to wake her to no avail. She had an outline of a hand across her cheek, another goose egg on the back of her head, and the beginnings of a black eye. Bastards! How could they do this to a woman? How long was she caged?

Charlie and I continued our attempts at warming and waking her for the rest of the ride. She needed electric warming blankets and warming fluids I couldn't provide. At this stage, she needed to get to hospital.

# Chapter Nineteen

I gently handed Rosie over to Charlie beside me and jumped

out of the Rover, rounded the boot and opened the back door

of the vehicle. Reaching in, I grasped Rosie from under her

legs and around her back. Gently, I removed her, while

Charlie, held the Emergency Room door open. Once I was

through the door with her frozen body, Charlie wrapped the

blanket around my woman again.

While she trembled, I carried her to the Accident and

Emergency desk. Shivering was a good sign. The medical

staff quickly took her from me and began working on her. I

explained she had been kidnapped, and I was contacted for

rescue.

I called Sheelalgh and got Gracie's mobile number and rang her. On the first ring she connected as I calmly informed her, "Gracie, I have your mam back. She's being treated for a possible concussion and moderate hypothermia, since she was in the freezing water for so long."

"Oh my God, will she be alright," she queried through her sniveling.

"Yes, pet, she'll be fine. They're working on warming her up."

"Can I talk to her," she asked.

"Not right now, I'm in the waiting room at Emergency. They're getting her out of her wet clothes and under some warming blankets. They'll run a warming intravenous drip to warm her from the inside too. She'll be grand, she just needs time."

"Oh. Okay. What do I need to do? Can I come down there now," she inquired.

"No, not yet. Stay there and if not tonight, I'll order Callum and Ian bring you to her at hospital first thing in the morning. Please don't leave without them. I'll let you know as soon as she's awake and allowed visitors."

"Okay. Thank you, Liam. Are you sure she's okay?" she asked again.

"No worries, pet. I've seen this a hundred times. Your mam's a tough lady. She just needs to warm up."

"Alright. Thanks again, Liam, and take care of my mom. Tell her I love her and I'm calling Opal and Lilly," she told me.

"Alright, will do. Gracie, I understand you've been waiting all day, it took a bit longer than we thought. Thank you." I ended the call

I sat outside in the waiting room with Simon and Charlie for what seemed like forever. At some point, Simon ushered me into a storage closet and removed the bullet. He stitched me up like he does everyone else. Out of all my men, he's my best medic by far. His stitching is remarkable. Charlie brought in my go-bag, Kian had dropped to Hospital for me. After changing into dry clothes, and what seemed like an eternity, they allowed me into Rosie's room.

All sorts of warm fluids were being intravenously injected into her body with warming blankets wrapped around her. She had Moderate Stage Hypothermia and a Mild Concussion, just as we all thought. I sat in the chair next to her with my hand on top of hers, under the warming blanket. After another two hours, she woke up.

Gazing over at her pale face, I and smiled and whispered, "Hi Dearheart."

"Hi Handsome," she greeted me.

I took her hearing aid box out of my pocket and held it up to her. She reluctantly lifted her hands out from under her warming blankets as I placed it in her hand. Pressing a button on the box, she attempted to find her abutment on her skull. She was so weak, she couldn't snap it on. Gently brushing her wet hair out of the way I took it from her. I snapped it to her head and waited for her. After a few seconds, she smiled and weakly said, "Thank you, I can hear you now."

"You had a rough go of it and scared the Devil out of me, Darling. I came to rescue you and you jumped out the balcony and killed a Muckle of a man. Simon and I yelled, but you just took off like a bat-out-of-hell. Why?" I asked short chuckles shaking my head.

"That *was* you. I wasn't sure as I had lost my hearing aid. We have to find Gracie now, Liam. Someone named Cronus has her," she croaked in desperation but too weak to move. I smiled down at her and said,

"I'm Cronus, Darling." She glanced up at me with wide eyes in disbelief and weakly asked,

"What?"

"I'm Cronus. I have Gracie. I got her back the next day with Peters help. She's fine, and she's at the hotel with Callum and Ian. They'll bring her by in the morning, or tonight if you want. Just tell me what you want." After a moment of contemplation, she gazed up at me and said,

"If Gracie's safe, then I want you to hold me, Liam. Hold me and never let me go."

I moved to the opposite side of the bed to not wanting
to dislodge her warming fluids, and gently did as she
requested. Moving her over to the side of the hospital bed
after I wrapped her back under the warming blanket. What she
doesn't realize is that I *am* never letting her go. I'll spend the
rest of my life protecting her and loving her.

After I snuggled in and kissed her head, she passed
out, again. I wrapped her tighter in the warming blanket and
snuggled up next to her. I kissed her on the forehead, cheeks,
and chin. I held her in my arms and nuzzled my lips on her
head while I held her. Her hair was reekin. It stunk like a
combination of seaweed and new carpet chemicals. I took my
mobile out and rang Gracie, informing her that Rosie did wake
up and is asleep again. The doctors were not saying anything
yet, but I'll let her know when they do, or she can come by in
a few hours."

A nurse walked in insisting I get out of the bed. I ended the call and growled at the nurse, threatening her within an inch of her life if I'm removed from this bed. She left us alone after that and never entered the room again.

A good hour later, Rosie woke back up and gazed dreamily at me. I had fallen asleep and I woke up as she gently kissed my neck. What a wonderful feeling. Certainly, I didn't want her to stop, but I want to kiss her luscious full pink lips more.

I leaned down and lightly kissed her cheek by her ear. My lips lingered feather soft down her earlobe. Both of our breaths sped up. Moving across her soft cheek, again and again, I kept on with little kisses. My hot breath was on her skin as I continued, ever so slowly to kiss my way to her mouth. I stopped at her mouth, begging her to take control. My heart thumped out of my chest in anticipation.

Rosie gazed up at me smiling and gently held the side of my face in her warm palm as she closed her eyes, and brushed her hot lower lip over my top lip. I could feel her breath on me as the touch of her mouth was feathery-light. Slowly, she lowered her mouth down to my lower lip and lightly did the same, the sensuality made my toes curl. Ever so passionately, she kissed my lower lip and for a fraction of a second, lightly sucked it into her mouth and moaned. Unfurling every sense as it was the most intimate experience of my life. No speed, no consumption, only passion.

Slowly, she moved up and kissed me so innocently on both lips. Claiming my mouth with her open lips. Each kiss more and more intense as she made little kitten sounds. Hungry, she ran her tongue lightly over the seam of my lips as I held the back of her head at her neck as we consumed each other. For several long minutes, we were lost in ecstasy, as only Rosie and I existed in our own world.

As she broke from my lips, she gazed up at me weakly and smiled. After a few short minutes of gazing at each other in adoration, breathing each other in, with our mouths millimeters away, her eyes disconnected with mine. Her smile faded and she spoke.

"Honey, they showed me a picture of a sculpture."

I had to regain my composure promptly and added, "Aye, Helmsmeier owed the Mob a sculpture. It came out in the briefing at Base, remember."

"The sculpture is at my parents' house, in the family room. It lays next to the Buddha head my Dad brought back from Nepal. My grandfather bought the statue while he was in Greece. It is the headless body of a woman cast in bronze, but its patina makes it look black," she informed me.

"Would your parents be home?"

"Maybe not. They travel a lot to their vacation homes during May," she said.

I quickly pulled the mobile from the pocket of my trousers and rang Aisling. She picked up on the second ring and asked, "What's the craic, Joe?"

"Cronus."

"Yes Sir."

"You and Cat take Lilly to her grandparents and collect that metal statue of a naked woman their Granddad brought back from Greece. Lilly should know the one. Rosie says is in their Livingroom by the Buddha head from Nepal. Don't call ahead, in case their lines are tapped. Pick the lock if Lilly doesn't have a key. Bring the statue back to Belfast with you after your detail ends. I'll have the jet bring you back.

"If Roses parents are home, take them outside away from the house and cars and tell them about the statue. Don't say anything about the painting yet. I have Rose here and Gracie's at the hotel. Tell Lilly they're both grand. Check the house, cars, mobiles and landlines for bugs."

I glanced down at Rosie, and she was fast asleep again. I held her in my arms until she awoke and kissed me all over again. I'll never tire of kissing my woman.

A knock sounded at the door. A Dutch Police Officer walked into the room and announced, "We're here to question Ms. Kelly, Sir. Please, would you step outside, so we can begin, that would be appreciated?

Rosie peered up from her slumber at the officer standing at the foot of the hospital bed. Striking out her chin in defiance she challenged, "No. He's not leaving me *ever*".

"Ma'am. He cannot stay. He has to leave," the officer lifted his palm up calmly stating.

Rosie stared up at him again with a venomous look on her face, bore her teeth, growled, raising her voice she stated, "I'm exhausted, in pain, and I'm done. He's not leaving me."

"Ma'am, that is not possible. Protocol states," he argued.

She quickly interrupted him and scoffed. Throwing her arm out from under the warming blanket and raising her voice she commanded, "*Fuck* your protocol. He didn't do this to me. He rescued me. I was kidnapped on Sunday, trying to bring my daughter back. *She* was kidnapped Saturday morning." The officer shook his head and paused in thought for a moment. Continuing, he said,

"Against, my better judgment, let's go through what happened then *I'll decide*." Temporarily pacifying her. Rosie was wide awake. Trying not to smile as she was so adorable angry, I passed her a cup of warm tea before she began her statement. *That was so hot!*

"Friday night, my home outside Belfast was broken into. Four men killed my dog and destroyed my home looking for my Grandfather's painting. I can send you the police report if you need it." The officer nodded as Rosie continued,

"Saturday morning, I received word my daughter hadn't returned home from her night out with friends. Following that, I received a call, from a computerized voice. He instructed me to take my Grandfather's painting to the Van Gough in exchange for my daughter. If I didn't or if I contacted the police, he would *kill* my daughter. You can check my call log when I go back to the hotel if you like.

"With my partner's help here, we were at the Museum. The kidnappers lured me away from my partner, Liam, trying to take the painting without exchanging my daughter. I fought them and I fought them *hard*. They took me and the painting to where they held my daughter. They were violent, exceptionally violent, and how I got these bruises. I guess the German Mob was trying to kill Helmsmeier, the mastermind, and attacked them. See this tracker?" Rosie leaned over and pointed to the tracker on the top of the bedside locker.

"I ran down the pier and jumped in the water with my daughter. My partner here, Liam, found where we were taken, watched us jump in the water, and swam to us. With *one* foot might I add? He was able to collect my daughter out first, but the tide was going out. I hit the current and was swept away. Liam found me before I drowned. I was in the water for over an hour. It's how I got here. Liam brought me here.

"You shouldn't be asking him to leave. You should be thanking him because you didn't have to pull *my dead body* out of the ocean!" She demanded to force him to back down. The officer turned to me and asked,

"Is that what happened, Sir?" I responded nodding my head,

"Aye." The officer pulled the other chair over and asked her to repeat the happenings, and she did, while he took notes. Later, he asked me and I verified Rosie's story. The officer turned to leave and asked us to stay local, but Rosie crossed her arms over her chest, pinched her lips together interjecting,

"No, I'm going home as soon as I'm released. My daughter is safe and has mock exams next week at the University. If you need a written statement, I'll email you one

from the Police Service at home." She gave him her mobile number and finally, he left.

That was easier than I thought it would be. I peered down at Rosie and whispered, "Why did you cover for me, Dearheart?"

"Why wouldn't I. I couldn't tell them we killed people. I want to spend my future *with* you, not with both of us behind bars. I was already thinking of an excuse for the bruises." Shaking her head, she confessed, "Being down this road before, and I knew exactly what they thought. When you live with a violent man, you start making excuses off the cuff like old hat."

I didn't like her answer, but I appreciated it and nodded.

Another knock at the door sounded and a herd of doctors came in. I immediately got off the bed and moved to the far wall, so they could assess her. The primary physician instructed the nurses to remove the blanket, and stop the warming intravenous drip. Instructing further to continue monitoring Rosie's core temperature and as long as she maintained her temperature, she'd be released in a little while. Her doctor instructed her to wrap herself in blankets and make sure to drink warm liquids for the next 24 hours. She kept trying to convince the doctor a steady stream of hot-toddies would do. I could only shake my head and laugh with the doctor.

After the herd of doctors and nurses' unplugged Rosie and left, she patted the bed for me to snuggle up with her again, but on the other side. I did, of course as I didn't want to be apart from her. I never wanted to be apart from her again. Once I had her snuggled in, she pointed to my chest and informed me,

"*This* is my snuggle spot. This is all mine. *You're* all mine." I lowered my head down to her smiling and jokingly said,

"Does this mean you'll go out to supper with me Saturday night?"

"Handsome, I'm yours every night." She whispered, with a huge smile, nodded her head, and then pulled me in by my shirt for another long kiss. I held the back of her head and deepened the kiss and for long minutes we were lost in each other. Tongues tangled, lips nipped, sucked, and swollen. Long minutes later, with Rosie literally melting in my arms, someone cleared their throat.

Gracie was here, smiling with Callum, Ian, and Charlie who had taken over guard duty for Simon. Rosie looked over at Gracie and beamed, and held out her arm for a hug. I swiftly adjusted myself before I stood by the bed. I let Gracie take over my spot on the bed. The girls hugged each other and Gracie cried. Rose didn't go into her second kidnapping of the day. She stuck to the story she told the Dutch Police officer. Grace was upset enough, she didn't need anything else on her shoulders.

"I called Opal and Lilly. They said they'd talk to us all tonight. You're coming back to the hotel, right?"

"Yes, I think that would be best for tonight. You want to snuggle up with me tonight and keep me warm?" Rosie suggested as she smiled at her daughter.

"Yes, I'll keep you, warm mom. Now that you're back, though, I have mock exams next week, and I should start studying tomorrow. I couldn't exactly do it this week. I might need you to call into the University and tell them what happened." She advised.

"Yes, I'm sure the Dutch police will want to talk to you too. We'll need to go over our story about your rescue before you do that, though. What happened?" Rosie asked both Grace and me.

"Go ahead and tell her Gracie," I said urging her on smiling. *Hearing her point of view would be fun.*

Grace sat up on the bed and explained, "After Helmsmeier got me out of the bed at the house, and he took me to the helipad outside. We got in this big helicopter, not a small one, like the news uses. We flew for a long time and I puked all over the floor." She went on, after we stopped laughing hysterically.

"We landed with another helicopter at the Brewery, Grandma always takes me to buy their beer. He walked me into the woods to a Grotto, which I never even knew they had, and handed me off to Liam. They yelled at each other for a while, and the gunshots in the field by the Brewery.

Helmsmeier ran, and Liam took my hand and I went with him

back through the woods to the Rectory. We've never been in

the Rectory, though, so I ran Liam to the Brewery, because

that had a basement.

"We got in fine and I got to see Father Peter. He gave

me a big hug. Did you know, he and Liam are best friends?

Liam gave me his .09 mm from his ankle holster, so I went to

the window to shoot with Father Peter. He didn't have a gun,

though, you know. Right after I got to the window, the last

guy was down, though. I didn't kill anyone.

Probably a good thing, I suppose. I don't want to kill

anyone, but I will stop someone from killing me. I have a right

to protect my person, and they were shooting at us. But Liam's

men killed them all. Helmsmeier killed himself in the

helicopter. Liam's men took care of all the bodies and cleaned

up, though.

"Father Peter said he'll ship Grandma their ale from now on. Anytime we want to stop in and say hi, he said we're welcome to. He wants to meet you too, mom. Liam's helicopter is way bigger than Helmsmeier's. I threw up in the garbage bag, then fell asleep. We got back to the airport and drove to the hotel. I sat down with Liam at the hotel, and we ate, although I did drink a whole bottle of pink Moscato and another bottle today," she said as we all had another good laugh.

"We went over everything, and we figured where the house was on the waterfront. I stayed at the hotel ever since. I got you a bunch of dark chocolate from the store downstairs and a gorgeous diamond broach. It has real diamonds, mom. Ian said I could buy whatever I wanted."

We all laughed as Gracie went through pretty much everything. I went into the hall for a few minutes and spoke to

Charlie and grabbed some fizzy juice for us from the machine. I wanted to give the girls some privacy for a little while.

Ten minutes later, Gracie left with Callum and Ian in tow. I walked back into the room and snuggled with Rosie on the bed. She turned to me and said, "You gave my twenty-year-old, blue-haired daughter a handgun, but not me, huh?"

"I realized how wrong I was when you were running down the pavement between the museums. I should have given you one. I was wrong, and I am so sorry for that," I stated.

"At the Brewery, when Grace asked me for a gun or a crossbow, I gave her my extra piece. She amazed me as she completed all the safety checks before she took off toward the window. I should have never hindered you from protecting yourself, I'm sorry." I said as I looked down at her waiting for her forgiveness.

"You're forgiven. But don't do it again. I practiced with most of your guns in the Armory at some point, even the sniper rifles. Trust is a two-way street, buddy," she said with a smile.

"I talked to Grace about your time with her in the waterfront house. Gracie told me you were studying the tides and you had a plan to dive in, but I thought I would reach you before that. What happened to make you jump?"

"The guards panicked knowing the German Mob was coming after them for some statue Helmsmeier owed them. They didn't think Helmsmeier would be back before they attacked. Whoever the German Mob is, they're violent and kill everyone in sight, so they prepared to leave. They need a better name than Der Mob, by the way. It sounds ignorant." She said, with a chuckle. I informed her,

"Yes, they're the German Mob, but they're part of the Italian Mafia, and have been for some time. We've had a few run-ins with them. I believe they took you the second time."

She hesitated, looking me in the eye for a brief moment and continued,

"The ape wouldn't let me go, he was afraid Helmsmeier would kill him if he did. I yelled at him and said that I wasn't leaving the house, and he should go. He disagreed, and we both thought it was the Mob's men with all the gunfire. You had four men with you last time, and there was much more commotion going on downstairs than four men could warrant, Handsome," she continued.

"It had to fight now or die and if I'm dying, I'm going down in a blaze of glory, so I charged him from across the room and it worked, he softened the blow. The tide was beginning to go out, like I had been observing and I thought that was my best chance. Some villain named Cronus had my daughter and I had to get out to get to you. Knowing this, would you have done differently?"

"No. I would have done the same. You're amazing, you know that? The most amazing woman I've ever known." Rosie raised her head to me with a smirk and said,

"You're just a smooth-talker you know that?" she said. I leaned down and ran my lips over her outer left ear and said,

"Darling, you haven't seen anything yet." Making a growling noise, I gently bit her neck, right where I kissed her yesterday morning. Rosie giggled as I found her magic spot, as she squirmed, she held on to my upper arm and felt my bandage. Immediately she lost her smile, and asked,

"Handsome, what happened to your arm?"

"Aye, Simon patched me up a bit ago."

"You have a medic on your team?" She questioned, looking up at me with concern in her eyes.

"Darling, we're all trained medics, snipers, and other things you don't want to know about." Hugging her close as she nestled her nose into my neck and sighed. I was never letting this woman go. After a few moments, with her arms still around my neck, she leaned back, looked at me and said,

"I wanted to kiss you the other day, before we went to the Museum, but I wanted the timing to be right." She admitted.

"Aye, I thought you did," I said smiling.

"The Beards occupied the Livingroom and it just didn't feel like the right time. Tensions were too high with what just happened in the bathroom and the exchange that night. I've wanted you for so long. Since you started coming into the cafe really, but I was afraid. Afraid to let someone else in that door

and afraid to get my heart broken again. I was so broken after

Ciaran. I didn't think I would ever move past it.

"Low and behold, you walked in and opened that door.

Thank you for walking through that door to me, Liam. Thank

you for being patient with me, even though I pushed you

away. Every time you would talk to me at the cafe or you

would look at me I felt like I couldn't breathe. I could barely

look at you, you're so handsome. It's why I call only you that.

You are the most handsome man I've ever seen, Liam. When

you touch me, even in the slightest way, I melt into a puddle.

You slowly warmed my heart up and awakened something in

me, I thought I had lost. Please don't let go. Give us a chance,

she said as I silent tear glided down her face."

She licked her lips, placing her palm on my chin

looked at my mouth, leaned up, and kissed me sweetly. I

closed my eyes, kissed her long and hard and vowed,

"I promise you, Darling, I am *never* letting you go."

"Will you tell me what happened on the boat," I asked. She nodded, then began.

"As I came up to the surface to breathe, I thought I heard you. Then someone grabbed my legs from below. Talk about a nightmare come true. He grabbed hold of me and pulled me under the water, and he wouldn't let me go no matter how hard I kicked. We resurfaced and he took off his rebreather. He said, if I made a sound, I'd die. He pulled out another rebreather and handed it to me. We dove underwater for what seemed like forever until we came upon the yacht.

"I barely made it up on the swim platform, I was so cold. There were three other men, and they grabbed me under the arms and threw me down the stairs into the cabin. I landed on the galley floor. They argued amongst themselves quite a bit and kept yelling at me in some foreign language. I signed that I'm deaf, but they didn't understand. They gave me a pen and paper and I wrote down that I'm deaf, and they laughed at me. Ignorant morons, is what they were. The thug with the big gold chain showed me a picture of the statue on his cell phone. I wrote down that I never saw the statue. He slapped me then.

"After they left the cabin, I went through the drawers and found the flare gun and some flares. I stuffed them in the back of my jeans. I was going to go for the kitchen drawers to look for a knife, but the thug with the gold chain saw me. Lashing out, he punched me again in the face. I hit my head and I must have passed out. I woke up later and we had stopped. Standing, I looked out the window, to see where we were, and I saw an explosion, and he decked me again. That's the last thing I remember. Did you find the flare gun or did they take it off me?"

"There isn't one here, so no," I answered her.

"I looked for what I knew, from boating so long with my family and Ciaran. I did the best I could. I didn't think I could overcome them and jump in the water. Especially since they had a diver, and I was so cold; but if we were in port, as I had seen at the end, I could create enough of a disturbance with the flare gun to move everyone out of the cabin. That could be my chance to run. It's probably why he knocked me out."

"You're so strong, do you know that? You'd been kidnapped, nearly drowned, and were beaten and you were still trying to save yourself."

"Call it what you want. I had to get to you and Gracie. I couldn't lay down and die. You had to know Cronus had her. I feel silly saying that now. You had her all along. When I was eating stale dinner at the house, you were out with your men and Peter risking your lives to bring Gracie back to me. I was just fine. You were the one that was out there on your own. I wish I would have realized you were Cronus from the beginning. I never would have jumped out that window, Sweetheart."

I took her face in both my hands and looked her in the eye making sure she heard me. "Dearheart, I'm going to call you amazing and strong and fierce, because you are all of those things. I'm so sorry you went through all of that. You shouldna been taken and that's that. It's my fault."

"No Liam, false guilt is what they call that. Neither you nor I are responsible for what someone else does. It is hard to grasp and let go. I work on mine all the time. Alright?"

"Aye. What about the cage?"

"What cage?" she asked becoming concerned.

"When Riley found you, you were locked in a cage under the v-berth and pulled you out"

"No, I don't remember a cage. Maybe that's a good thing."

"Aye, let me know if you do, okay? We'll get through it together. "

"You'll have to tell me what kind of treats, or cakes and pies Riley likes." She stated.

"Why does Riley get treats and not me?"

"Riley pulled me out of a cage you said."

"Aye, he got there first, but I held the cage open, so he could lift you out." She looked at me and grinned. And said,

"Are you jealous of Riley's treats? I'm only making him a few treats, but Handsome, you get all the best treats." She said as she kissed my lips. "The special treats." She kissed my lips again. "The sexy treats." She kissed me again.

"Well, in that case." I said as I deepened our kiss.

# Chapter Twenty

The doctor released Rosie an hour later. Charlie and Simon

drove us back to the hotel, and had already ordered dinner. On

the way back, Rosie swore me and the guys to silence about

the thug attacking her in the bathroom, and the German Mob

kidnapping her, and the cage. She *ordered* me to inform my

men, as they might bring it up in front of Grace.


   I prepared Rosie a hot bath with her lavender salts, in

the bathtub in my room, not hers. I even brought scented

candles in and another hot-toddy. She said she never wanted

to use the other bathroom again. I didn't blame her, but I really

wanted her to wash her reekin hair. I collected her big bottle

of shampoo and hairbrush she brought from home, placing

them in the bathtub as a subtle reminder. She was scunnered, bruised, and broken. Determined, I needed to expel her pain, anyway that I could.

I wanted to make her better and offered to help her wash her bogging hair, but she said not with Grace here. Save that for our time, back home. That wasn't thinking of that, but she's right. It would not be appropriate with Grace here. I need to change my way of thinking. I need to consider the girls now, with them in my life. Grace lay on my bed reading, just in case her mom needed any help. I needed to change my mindset of having three grown children. As it is, I will always protect them with everything in me.

Shortly after my two girls situated themselves, I entered Poseidon's room for debriefing, Riley brought in Sheelagh on video chat who informed us on the investigation. The Dutch Police believe Helmsmeier's men made the hit on the yacht, prompting the takedown at the compound and explosion. Hopefully, with the tangos in the cold drink, they won't realize they died over two hours after.

The Dutch Police raided the waterfront compound soon after we left for Almere Poort. Sheelagh received Intel that the police are blaming the German Mob for all of it. It is common knowledge with the police force they were hunting Helmsmeier and had been for some time.

Grace went gangbusters in the shop downstairs having Callum buy everything from chocolates and shoes to expensive jewelry. As long as it was for my girls, I was happy. We ate dinner on the sofa laughing and drinking a bit too much. Rosie nursed a steady stream of hot-toddies, while we all participated in the video chat with Opal and Lilly.

All three of Rose's girls are adorably jubilant. Their personalities are all exceptionally diverse, although they all looked alike. One thing I noticed about all the girls is they share their Mother's adorable dimples that only shown when they smiled. All three had turned up little button noses and Rosie's beautiful blue eyes, and as they smiled, they all lit up like sunshine. When all four of the girls are together, they are a magnificent sight to see. They are so connected and in tune with each other. I was truly astounded.

Every other word out of Opal's mouth is a curse word and her normally brown hair is currently dyed silver, with a turquoise sheen underneath. I can't even imagine how that color was crafted. She's only eighteen, and Rosie said she's just having fun being young, and to let her get it out of her system, before she's forced to join the workforce in the real world. Opal taught her female bodyguards of Team Three sign language, and how to play the ukulele. She also made them dinner every night. It sounded like they greatly enjoyed each other's company.

She said she would be home from Munich after her University is released in June. She couldn't wait to meet her mam's "new beau" as she called me. She requested to have us all together for one of her mam's home-cooked Sunday dinners at the Lough House.

I found out Rosie calls Lilly, Lilly Belle, after her favorite cartoon movie character. Lilly, who is twenty-four, hasn't changed her hair from dark blonde. She's in University back in Ohio. She appeared to be getting along well with one of her bodyguards, Aisling. She was routinely sent out to purchase bottles of her favorite wine. She said Aisling and Cat both gained a half-stone from her constant cooking and baking.

Lilly has a small group of friends that bake different kinds of artisan bread. They deliver them all to each other weekly. Aisling had been given chauffeur duty.

Lilly is thrilled with her protection detail. She's not happy she couldn't know which celebrities the Erebus Teams protected. She joined the video chat from the Rover while Aisling and Cat took turns driving her up to Rosie's parents' home to collect the statue.

We stayed the night in Amsterdam as Rosie needed to recover, and we all needed to catch up on sleep. More importantly, because Gracie needed time with her mam, which I was more than happy to provide. Before she joined Grace in her bedroom, Rosie pulled me into my bedroom, shut the door, and pushed me to the wall, and winched the life out of me. My woman has a wicked nip. She was definitely feeling better and I cannot wait to take her home. She's unleashed her inner sex goddess. She needed to allow her body to heal build up her strength first.

Rosie met with each team and thanked them personally. Turned out, she already knew most of them from the cafe. Rosie had changed into a non-vulgar shirt, thankfully.

I sent all the Teams home at 0600, excluding Callum and Ian. After breakfast, Rosie and I drove Gracie, home to her apartment, and said our goodbyes. She had mock exams the following week she couldn't miss. I left Callum and Ian to protect her for the following three weeks of school, just in case of an unknown blowback. She appreciated the knowledge being tailed on her yellow motorbike. She was also contacting her therapist and continuing her specialized trauma therapy again.

We headed to the airport and boarded to make our way home. Without Bravo on the jet, it was quiet. While I was backed up on work, I had to log in for at least an hour responding to urgent messages. When I closed my laptop, I swiftly slid my laptop in my bag. When I sat back up, Rosie jumped onto my lap straddled me, and we let loose snogging like teenagers. Rosie calls me her Snuggle Bunny. I informed her she can call me anything she wants, as long as my men don't hear it. She laughed and joked for a while, then, agreed it would hinder my authority at work.

We decided to keep the Amsterdam incident quiet. Rosie and I are both private people, and the fewer people that knew, the better. She was going to tell her parents and Kylie, though. She doesn't keep anything from them anymore.

Rosie was taking the rest of the week off to recover and put her house back together. At my request, she allowed a team from Kerberos to come over and help her. Although we did talk several times every day and every night before bed, she stated she needed space, temporarily. She needed to reassess her overprotective self and change her anxious behavior. She wasn't living her life to the fullest, and now understands, she can't predict the future.

She seemed to be doing fine without Pete by her side. I asked her if she wanted me to adopt a new dog for her, but she said no. She'd maybe like another one someday, but she didn't feel she needed one anymore. She was going to call her therapist, Lydia, and start her trauma sessions again, though. She expected having flashbacks and I agreed it was a wise choice.

We decided Saturday would be our first date. I wanted to make it sooner, but she needed more down time first. I had mountains of work to do and it preoccupied me until then.

# Chapter Twenty-One

Tonight, was our official first date. I planned on taking Rosie

to the Botanic Gardens, followed by dinner. This was the date

I planned for last Saturday. So much had happened in one

very long week. It was nice just to sit down and enjoy each

other's company for a change, with no looming drama, and I

never wanted to wait that long to see Rosie again.

Walking in her front door, and I was rendered

speechless. My breath speed up and I started to perspire. Rosie

wore a strapless, embroidered royal blue and black dress that

was so tight with her curves, it left little to the imagination.

She also wore sky-high diamond-studded ankle strapped

heels. Her long auburn hair was loosely curled and the sides

held back with diamond pins. I didn't think she wore jewelry, but tonight she displayed a huge diamond accent ring, tennis bracelet, and earring set. She also added her new diamond broach pinned to the side above her breast.

She must have covered her bruises in makeup, because I couldn't see a one. Never have I seen her this way before. Rosie has always been beautiful, but tonight, she was a *goddess*. I didn't know if I should strut her around town like a proud peacock, or cover her up and hide her away so no one else could steal what I have.

"Hiya, Handsome," she chimed walking down the foyer hall to me.

"You are delectable, Dearheart." She smiled and kissed me passionately for several long moments. She leaned into me, whispering in my ear.

"Thank you, so are you. I like your tie. I could do *a lot* with that," she said seductively running it through her fingers as she slowly slithered her hot lips down my neck. *Fucking hell, I can't breathe. I'm simultaneously on fire and frozen.*

"Now pick your jaw up off the floor, and let's get this show on the road," she ordered with a wink.

"You need to bring a jacket, I brought my bike," I informed her.

"No worries," she said and selected one off of the coat tree by the front door. "Are you going to be alright in that dress and shoes or do you want to take your motor," I asked as I helped her slide into her leather biker jacket.

She smirked at me and said, "No worries. My dress is too tight to go flying up. Besides, the weather is warm for once, and we need to enjoy it. My dad used to ride with me. I know how to avoid getting burned. Wait till you meet my mom, you'd never imagine she was his MC biker chick in the 70s." We laughed as we walked out to my bike.

She didn't mind the helmet on her red hair as the long ends shot like fire off the back of my custom ride. She held me tight, with her arms wrapped around my chest, *until* they drifted lower. At one point I reached my hand back to caress her sexy mile-long legs and felt the lace hem of her thigh-high stocking exposed. *Christ, I'll think about these all night with those shoes.*

We strolled through the Gardens always touching each other, making sure the other is close. We are connected, like nothing I ever experienced before. I can glance at her and know exactly what she is thinking or feeling. I couldn't help myself as I pulled her aside at one point, kissing her senseless behind the rubber trees. Although I had first date jitters like a teenager, I felt like we are much closer than that. After everything, we had been through together, we were. *Much* closer.

I took Rosie to the best romantic restaurant in Belfast. We sat intimately next to each other, instead of across the table. All through dinner, we laughed about anything and everything constantly touching each other. We shared our dinners with each other and dessert of triple chocolate ganache cake. I wiped chocolate off the side of my mouth, and she sucked it off my finger, I lost the battle right there. I never knew this side of her existed. I had hoped, but didn't know.

What I originally planned, with me being a gentleman and dropping her off at her the door will not be happening. Not with her in that dress, with thigh high stockings on. That and we need to clear the air once and for all to move forward. I needed her to open up and tell me everything that happened to her before we met.

My gut said there is way more to her story. Because her husband died before she bought this house, why did she have a £50k safe-room installed and why the courses at Kerberos. I thought long and hard on how to approach the subject. Like myself, she doesn't trust people as a rule. I trust her with everything in me, but if I hadn't earned her trust by now, I'm not sure how I would obtain it. To move us forward, I needed it.

After our dinner, back at her house, Rosie lit candles in the Livingroom. We snuggled on her re-assembled sofa on flipped over cushions. With our cocktails, I finally said, "Rose, you don't have to tell me, but, why you want to take a Close Quarters Battle Course?"

After a long pause she turned to me and nodded scooting back, she leaned against the sofa arm. She took off her shoes and extended her legs placing them on my lap, where I laid my hands on her feet, to comfort her with my touch. After making herself comfortable and taking another long drink, she began. "You're right, it is time. I have never told this to another man before; not knowing for sure when the time was right, but it is important to me that you know. It is a lot for someone else to take in. It's a long story, so I should probably start at the beginning if you're ready." I nodded and she began.

"My parents and siblings are wonderful, I had an amazing start. About age eighteen, I was sexually assaulted by a guy during a football game in high school. I had gone to get something from my car, and he came up behind me and pulled me down in-between the cars. He said if I told anyone, no one would believe me. He will come back and rape me again. I was so scared of him and ashamed. So much that, I kept it to myself. I didn't recognize him. Maybe he was from another school because he was around my age. I turned into myself and stopped going to school functions. No prom or any dances after that.

Two years later, at a frat party, I was forcibly pulled into a bathroom from behind and raped again by someone else. I told him I would tell the police, and he said go ahead, because they won't believe me. I guess his dad is a big crooked attorney. He played football and everyone adored him.

On Monday, I finally told the campus police two days later. They said since I already showered and there were no witnesses, nothing could be done. I had bruises on my inner thighs, arms, and chest, but they said that might be easily explained from rough sex. I mean, in those days, they gave us rape whistles at orientation. Times were different back then. I'm not sure they used DNA back in those days.

"I became afraid to go to class, go to the hall to eat, or leave my room. After two weeks of missing class, I called my parents, and they believed me. They transferred me to a local college and I lived at home. The words my attackers spoke damaged my integrity and created self-doubt. I felt tainted and a liar. To this day, I still know what happened. I remember what I wore when he pulled down between the cars in the parking lot. I still remember what I wore when he pulled me into the bathroom.

"You see, trauma forces you to remember things you wouldn't normally. It makes a permanent impression in your memory and as a result, made me hyper-aware of everything at all times. I became afraid to go places alone, since that's when they happened. Both of those men knew what they were doing. I still have problems going to big places alone. That's why I was so uncomfortable standing at the Promenade. You can't look behind you constantly, and I was a sitting duck. I wore the tee-shirt to mentally prepare myself.

"After college, I moved out of my parents and rented a tiny house. I met this guy through some of my friends, and we hung out as a group all the time. We had a lot of fun. We used to go to the bar in a big group and get drunk sometimes, well,

a lot of times. Joseph and I would dance together or talk. We

were not close like my other guy friends, though. We didn't

talk on the phone or hang out like I would with the others.

*They* were my brothers.

"One day, my mom called and asked me to come over.

When I sat down at her house, she asked who Joseph is, and I

told her. Then, she told me he showed up at the range and

introduced himself as my boyfriend. I said he's only a friend,

and we agreed it was odd. She asked me to stay away from

him, but I swear he was the sweetest guy and wouldn't hurt a

fly.

"Trust me, he did *not* go off on my Charles Mason

radar at all. I still wonder if he was actually the one, but there

is more. One night, not long after he approached my mother, I

heard a thump at my back door. I just had my first ear surgery

which left me deaf on the right side, and I doubted what I

heard. The thumping kept repeating for what seemed like forever. There wasn't a peephole to look out and no windows on that side. My vision didn't fail me because I saw the door flexing in. Someone was pushing on the door from the outside. I thought I must be dreaming. I had been asleep and the thumping woke me up.

"There's that self-doubt, creeping its way in again. I called the police and they found nothing. I went into the basement a few nights later to do laundry, and the window was wide open. I never, ever opened the basement windows, they were all nailed shut. The nail had been removed and laid on the concrete floor below. That only happened once, though.

"The thumping on the door happened a few more times, so my dad ordered an alarm installed at the house and I bought some door clubs. It took two weeks for the alarm to be installed. Each time when it happened, I just stood in the kitchen, with the police on the phone and the gun pointed at the door.

Dad said, if you pull your gun on someone, you best kill him. If you don't he'll take your gun and kill *you* with it. When you shoot him, make sure they step inside the house first. In case you shoot him before that, drag his ass inside. I was not going to be assaulted again. I will fight to the death. Not sleeping properly for weeks, I thought I was going crazy, because even with the alarm signs they gave me in advance; in the front yard, it didn't stop."

"Wait, you said the signs were in the front?"

"Yes," she answered.

"And he kept coming in the back?"

"Yes," she replied.

"He wasn't aware you had an alarm system, Love. Unless he drove by the front of your house all the time, he wouldn't have seen the garden signs."

"Well fuck me running." She muttered and we both broke out in laughter.

"One day, not too long after, Joseph knocked on my back door and told me he just bought the house behind mine and how much fun it would be now that we could hang around all the time. Of course, I never did. I never called him, never anything. I even stopped hanging out with those friends after he went into the range."

"At my parents' request, my landlord installed a new steel back door. Unfortunately, not with a peephole. The night my Grandmother passed away, my friend Angie came over to sit with me, and we cried and talked. She has always been such a great friend. She asked if I had heard voices because she could. I said no. I only heard the furnace kicking on. For a minute there, I wondered if she was slipping. Angie leaned over and peeped through the closed blinds, and spied several police cars in front of my house. I opened the door and asked what's going on. The officer told me nothing concerning me. Everything is fine, and go back inside, so I did.

"Two days later, I walked out to my car to attend the funeral. My nosey neighbor lady came out of her house in her bathrobe, and asked if the police caught those men. I had no idea what she was talking about. She told me she was up feeding her newborn when she witnessed two men trying to push in through my back door. She called the police. I never complained about nosey neighbors after that.

"I called the police station, and they said they never saw anyone. With my neighbor confirming everything, I knew I hadn't lost my mind, and that was *so* reassuring. I felt pretty confident after that, but the problems didn't stop.

"He got a temp job at my office. Of course, I ran to my boss, and he was let go that day. I mean, at that point, I started to keep my mom's favorite revolver in the glove box of my car. I also slept with it under the pillow at night. Being so paranoid, my friends volunteered to take me to the grocery store."

"Wait, you slept with a revolver under your pillow?"

"Yeah, well under the pillow next to me and facing away from me," she explained.

"Never do that, hen. That is not safe."

"What, you haven't done that," she questioned.

"No, I keep it on my bedside locker with the safety on."

"Well, I never owned a nightstand until I left Ciaran. There are two men that the police never caught. *Two men*," she excused.

"Come sit over here, Love," I said as I pulled her to my lap and wrapped my arms around her and listened.

"I started dating a high school teacher around about that time and everything stopped. Brendan come over at night, and we watched evening TV together and cook dinner. He would go home as we both had to work the next day. That only lasted a few months. I thought that was why the stalking stopped.

"Not long after I broke it off with him, I met Ciaran. We were head over heels. It was wonderful. He was so dashing. Everyone loved him. He was always the life of the party. He was in color. We both decided when my lease ended, I would move in with him and, transfer my job closer to his apartment across town. He was so charming, my mom called him my Knight in shining armor. Instead of a white horse and a sword, he had a white U-Haul truck and a pencil. What a joke.

I moved and within a month we eloped. Soon after that, everything changed. We moved to four hours away to Chicago for his job. He said this would make his career. He said I didn't need to work, his income would take care of us both. I insulted him when I wanted to continue my career. He had a big ego.

"I realized he was terribly selfish and controlling. Sometimes, he would come home half-drunk and beat up. He always came home with excuses, though. He stumbled upon a woman being mugged or walked into a bar fight, not meaning to. But nothing added up.

"He'd pick arguments with me over the stupidest things, like when I left two dishes in the sink. Then that progressed to both of us yelling, which began escalating to him throwing punches. For a long time I fought back, but it always made my physical pain worse. I escalated it by fighting back. It never stopped him. I loved him and I didn't ever want to hurt him. I reacted to his blows, trying to make him stop and get away from me.

"The gaslighting started after that. I wore too much make up, then not enough. I dressed too well, then let myself go. The house was never clean enough, even though I cleaned every day and twice when the girls were little. His clothes weren't hung the way he liked, so I laid them out every day for him to dress. If he didn't like what I laid out, he threw all the clothes on the floor from the hangers. At least once a week, that happened. He wanted to wear this white shirt and not that white shirt. He owned four of the same damn shirt in the same size. He really liked white shirts. He acted like a petulant child when things didn't go his way. So many things carried the same pattern. If he didn't like dinner, he threw his plate across the room and it smashed on the wall. If something was expired in the fridge, he threw each thing out smashing it violently on the kitchen floor. It was never-ending. Then the rapes started. Yes, you can rape your wife. I stopped having sex with him, and he would beat me into compliance. I disassociated during those times. It was too much.

"The constant gas-lighting never stopped, and I became very submissive. Finally, giving in, I did everything he said. The next thing, I faked my morning sickness. Who the hell can throw up on command? Until I had to be hospitalized and medicated he finally believed me. I could take the physical. What is hard is the emotional abuse. That messes with your head and cripples you. You are trapped. You are made to believe *you're* the bad one. It's *your* fault all of this is happening. He manipulated and coerced me. I thought I was going crazy.

"Quickly after we married, we had the girls and, I didn't think I would be able to support three little ones on my own. He kept throwing out my birth control pills, and they didn't have the shot back then. Three car seats and a triple stroller in tow. Nothing ever happened around the kids. After a while, the fighting stopped and things were fantastic for about two years.

"Then the paranoia started. One night, we were on our way home from the movies and someone followed us. He lost them, but later in the night, he told me this had been happening for a while. One morning, he went out to go to work and all the windows of his car had been smashed in. He finally told me these mob guys wanted him to launder money for him, and why he came home with the shiners. He had been laundering for them since we moved to Chicago.

"He wanted to go back home to Northern Ireland and be done with the laundering. We moved here eight years ago and everything went south again. Even though we had

liquidated all of our assets for the move, and paid cash for

everything nothing broke the trail. One year in, they found us

and everything started again. Our cars always smashed up,

suspicious phone calls...etc.

"I prayed a lot. More than ever. When you're at the

bottom, you realize God's all you've got. When things were

horrible, I used to pray for death. I found out he was having an

affair I confronted him, and he was violent for the last time. I

didn't even care he was cheating on me. I mean, we had

stopped having sex for about six months prior. I couldn't wrap

my head around the fact that he treated me worse than a dog,

then had the nerve to do that. I could have gotten *diseases*. I

won't go through it again, Liam, I can't. That marriage

certificate wasn't just a piece of paper, it was my death note.

"After his fifth restraining order and fourth arrest in

our marriage, I got down on my knees and prayed. I prayed

harder than I ever had before. I asked God to end this. Not in my death or his, but for God to show me and the girls a way out.

"Two days later I, saw an opening and I took it. We left for the last time. We had tried to go six times before, but he always found us and brought us back. Usually, I'd be kicking and screaming. He swore he was sorry, he loved us, and nothing would ever happen again.

"When we walked in-to the PSNI Police Station, I was black, blue, and we were all very broken. They took me and the girls to a Domestic Violence Safe House where we lived for six months. It was the most *important* six months of our lives. The house is hidden and gated, so I could park my car inside without worrying him or anyone else would see it. No one but the staff and other residents knew where we lived, just that we were safe.

"We walked a lot, usually on side streets. We changed phone numbers and made sure our cell phone and social media locations were all off. There was a whole process to go through if you choose. They encouraged me to contact our creditors and change bank accounts and mailing addresses. The bank, insurance company, and doctors all placed warnings on our accounts to not disclose information to Ciaran. My legal paperwork stated address confidential.

"They provided us specialized trauma counseling and abuse courses. I took them all, some of them I even took twice. Me and a room of middle and upper-class housewives. This can happen to anyone. A lot of great things came out of our stay, and we made some amazing lifelong friends, but most importantly I learned. I learned how and why this happened to me and how to make sure nothing ever happens again for myself and my girls. All of it started with the first rape which damaged me more than I realized. Self-care, and creating safe places for you to thrive in the present is the key. When we left the shelter, I was no longer broken.

"They gave me the glue and I put myself back together again, but I am still cracked. If you look closely, you can still see me through the cracks; I'm still here, just slightly obscured. They say it takes a village to raise a child, but really, it took a village to put us back together again. Between social workers, sexual trauma therapists, and all the classes, *we* are now whole again. I am no longer a victim. I am a *Survivor*. I weeded my garden and replanted my roses. They are more vivid than ever before.

"Ciaran died in his girlfriends' bed, back in Chicago by the time we left the shelter. I guess they were together off and on for nearly eight years. He flew over to Belfast for a time and put her up in a flat. *First-class.*

"I don't cry over it anymore. I've talked about the abuse so often between therapists and groups, it doesn't hurt as much. I removed myself from the past, yet, I am proactive in making sure *nothing* ever happens again. There are a lot of stereotypes, but abuse isn't exclusively with the fist. Abuse doesn't discriminate and can happen to anyone, by anyone. It has nothing to do with gender, race, or population. A wife, adult child, sibling, friend, partner, parent, grandparent and not just men. Most men don't behave this way. We need to build men's safe houses. There aren't enough. *They* are the *forgotten* victims. She exhaled and sighed.

I don't tell people about it anymore. No one. I told one of his family members that I was close with, and they abandoned me. Even some of my own family and friends abandoned me. They stopped talking to me and acted as if I was dirty and a liar. It was my fault, I was a troublemaker. The fact is, *he* was the dirty troublemaker. Losing my family hurt almost as much as what he did to me.

"All my skeletons are bared before you from my pad-locked closet. Did I overwhelm you? If you want to ask me anything, I am forever an open book to you. Would you like some more Scotch, you're, vibrating under me," she asked.

I exhaled, straightened my fingers from their balled fists, and held her tighter, kissing the top of her head. My sorrow wept down my face as I held her tight. She turned wrapping her arms tightly around me. Nuzzling into my neck giving me soft kisses in comfort. After a beat, I finally spoke through my silent tears.

"I am so proud of you. You are so strong. You are my wonderful-woman with her bulletproof bracelets, fighting off rounds one at a time." He moved his forearms up and mimicked "Ping. Ping. Ping." We chuckled and I kissed her forehead after she brushed my tears away. I held her tighter and rested my head on hers.

After a while, she spoke again "Thank you, Honey, but I don't think of myself as strong. Everyone says I am, but I am weak. I should have done more. I should have left him earlier, but I wouldn't have my kids. In class, we learned to call this false guilt, and I've not conquered it yet. I have taught my girls they can always be stronger, because you never know what's coming. I used to be fierce before the assault in high school. I used to own the room, now I only occupy it. Lydia says I'm still fierce. I'm still me, I need to find my fierceness and pull it out again."

"You are fierce, Love. The way you grabbed that thug's leg and held on at the museum was amazing. You jumped out of a two-story window and killed a man. You swam two miles in freezing water only to be beaten and nearly die of hypothermia on that boat. Did you not growl and curse at a Dutch Police officer? Honey, you are the fiercest woman I've ever known."

Changing the subject with a smirk I said, "I noticed that you swore and you didn't spell it."

"Yeah, I usually just swear in my head, but Mom's not fucking here."

We laughed for a bit, then, after, stretching my arms and yawning, as did my love. I told her, "You should write a book, aye. Someone may need the help and not know how to find it."

"Yeah, I've thought about it. A lot of people have told me that, actually. I'd have to use a pseudonym, though. I can't risk the Chicago Mob going after me again."

"It's up to you, let's go to bed, Love, I want to hold you in my arms all night."

# Chapter Twenty-Two

I woke up with Rosie wrapped my arms. Rosie was in her pink satin nightdress, and I was in my shorts from my go-bag, sans tee per Rosie's request. She prefers me without a shirt, all the time. With her story last night, I wasn't about to move things forward until she was ready. *And she was ready*. She shifted her butt back and squirmed against me, but I didn't have my leg on. "Stop," I whispered as I held her tighter. She squirmed again to test the waters and I held her tighter to me and muttered, "We can't, I don't have my leg on."

"Who cares," she mumbled.

"I care. I don't want you to see my stump without my leg on."

She turned around and sat up on her knees facing me half awake. She reached over and took her hearing aid off the bedside locker and snapped it on and began, "I dumped my huge bag of shit all over you last night, and we made love for two hours until I passed out. Do you think I'm worried about seeing your stump? I want to because it's part of you, Liam. I want to see the whole you, not just the part that you want people to. What if I need to help you with your prosthetic someday, huh? You no longer need to carry everything alone. I'm here, I'll carry you."

I scooted back so he leaned against the headboard. After rubbing my eyes and running my hands down my face, I finally asked "Aye, but why do you think you need to help me with it? My leg is my burden to carry, you have enough on your shoulders and I don't want to give you more."

She hesitated in thought. With a shy grin, she questioned me. "What if we take a bath or shower together, or we have hard and dirty for two hours one night. You pass out from exhaustion with your prosthetic on, and I need to remove it. I would need to be taught how. Sweetheart. You shouldn't sleep with your leg on anyway, that couldn't be comfy. Are you going to make me search on the internet after sex?"

I laughed and evaded the leg issue asking, "You like hard and dirty for two hours?"

"Who doesn't, *we* could break my record!" She exclaimed all excited and her face lit up with a huge smile. She was back to herself with her beamer. Rosie unencumbered is a sight to behold, and I love it.

"Wait. Hold on a minute." I smiled holding my palm up. "You have a two-hour hard and dirty record?" I questioned with a smile.

"What? No, I have an *orgasm* record. Every woman does," she explained as she waved her hand off to me.

"Every woman has one?"

"Of course. I own a big bag of tricks and I could *make* you show me," she advised with a smirk and a wink. "I'm going to take a quick shower and brush my teeth. After I'm done, tell me your decision." She got off the bed, scurrying to the shower.

Realizing I lost that battle, but was about to come out winning regardless. I had already decided to concede, as I stripped out of my athletic shorts. She was right, and I knew that I needed to share my brokenness. I always planned to, I hadn't thought ahead past last night is all. My brain was mush by the time we finished making love. I barely got my lower leg off before I passed out myself. Being with Rosie is a dream come true. She's overcome so much, mine feels somewhat different in comparison.

I heard the water shut off and Rosie walked into the room naked. I threw back the duvet, completely exposed, and said.

"How about you give that a go, Love." She grinned, quickly skirted to the bed on her belly, and *blew my mind*. We made love for two more hours. I *definitely* broke her orgasm record.

#

Three hours later, we finally emerged from the bedroom, after a long bubble bath, ready for our day, or should I say early afternoon. Thankfully, Rosie took a few extra days off after all that excitement. She needed her strength for last night and this morning.

"I owe you a check, Dearheart. Sheelagh texted a bit ago and your theories were right about the vault heist"

"SHUT-UP," she exclaimed in disbelief as her mouth hung open.

"No, seriously. The tunnels did lead to the bank and old courthouse basements, as well as all the other buildings in that row. The padlock to the tunnel entrance in the park was freshly cut. Someone or someone's, took a pickax, and chipped out a person size hole in the old stone tunnel. Just like you said.

From their best guess, they also used a cordless hand saw to cut out the wall and pulled out a ton of horsehair. I guess they used it as insulation back then. Who knew? They got in and out through there, then closed up the hole with brand-new Sheetrock. See these pictures, they made a shite mess of it too." I told her as I flipped through the pictures on my mobile

"Look. The Sheetrock isn't even close to being as big as the hole, and they used duct tape and putty to fill in the gaps. They did everything outside the vault without gloves, so the PSNI collected new fingerprints. They also found a freshly chewed piece of gum and the pickax at the bottom of the pile of the horsehair about six feet from the hole, so they collected DNA. Guess who the fingerprints matched?"

"My top suspects would be an employee or vault cleaner," she stated.

"It was the vault cleaner. The PSNI discounted his prints before, since he was considered staff."

Rosie turned to me astonished and said, "Wow. That's amazing! How stupid they were. People think they can get away with this stuff. If there was a fool-proof way to rob a bank, everyone would."

We laughed and laughed. I picked her up and placed her on the counter. I spread her legs apart and stood in-between them, holding her shapely bum in my hands, I asked. "How did you know about the old tunnels, I didn't have any idea they were there?" She looked at me and explained.

"Gracie and I took a Paranormal Ghost Hunt Tour at Halloween one year, when she was really into those shows on TV. The tour cost a small fortune. They scheduled six hours but at hour four, we cut out. They told us all about the tunnels and the entrance-way in the park. Sorry, I forgot to tell you where it was. They walked us through the basement of the Courthouse to show us the cells and the entrance door to the tunnels. The cells were tiny and still had shackles on the walls.

We didn't go into the tunnels, though, because of the rats, and they're just gross."

I leaned closer and lightly ran the tip of my nose down her neck and whispered with my hot breath. "How did you know look at the false ceiling and toilets?"

"That vault heist happened back in the States. The police didn't have *any* clues, then they finally caught some guy in an unrelated daytime robbery. He was responsible for a whole slew of bank robberies and was going to be given something like five back-to-back life sentences, so he made a deal to receive a lower prison term. He confessed to the vault heist, and told the police exactly how he did it as part of his deal. I didn't pull that out of thin air. You need to use every bit of knowledge you hold in your arsenal to figure it out. *You* are fully aware of this, Cronus", she teased.

I kissed her long and hard. When I broke the kiss, I put my forehead to hers and said, "You know I love ye, right?"

"Yes, I know." She said with a smile on her face.

"You do?" I asked, smiling.

"Yes, I do. I love you too. I love you more than I've *ever* loved anyone." She told me smiling in return.

I took her face in my hands and kissed her passionately, with long intense strokes. Our kisses keep getting better and better. After pulling back from our kiss, she said, "I don't want that money and I owe you a check for saving Grace and I from that German lunatic."

"You owe me nothing and you'll take that money."

"Liam, I have £1.2M between my savings accounts and investments," she said. I still had my arms around her waist but leaned back, looked at her in the eye and said,

"What? You drive a ten-year-old jeep. Where did you shake that kind of money, Love?"

"I won the lottery about three months after Ciaran died. And my jeep is old, but she still runs. And before you ask, no, I didn't kill Ciaran. I did pray daily to Saint Rita, though, for intercession hoping God would take him out. I'm not saying he killed him for me, but that man isn't breathing anymore. I consider it a win.

"That's how I bought the coffee shop, this house, and the Lough house. Not just that, but also how I put my girls through University in three different countries. University education is not cheap overseas and neither is their housing. Sweetheart, I've had the $700 per month new car payment.

I've had the biggest house on the street. I didn't need that then and I don't need that now. I'd rather have the money in the bank." She said shaking her head.

"Well I'm glad you have that and I will never want to be on your bad side," I said with a laugh.

"Are you hungry, Sugar?" I asked her poking my mamma bear.

"Starved, I'll put on the music while you find out what we have in the fridge."

*I won. We danced and I serenaded her while we cooked. Together.*

# Chapter Twenty-Three
One Year Later

I gazed out to the Lough admiring the late evening sailboats with The Mourne Mountains in the background. The sun was just setting and the Cooley Mountains around us were blocking the sunset. This is truly a breathtaking spot. We spend every weekend we were able here, together. I have moved in with Rosie permanently, as per her request. Her house is bigger anyway. We need space for both of us and the girls. We renovated the spare first-floor bedroom into my office as I found myself working from home more often. I use mine as a safe-house for clients until we decide to sell it. We make all our financial decisions together nowadays. We've had a jam-packed wild ride this year with the girls and Kylie.

She's our fourth daughter and gave us our first Granddaughter. I'm proud to call all four of them that. I may not have given them life, but as Rosie taught me, they all make my life better.

I was nervous about proposing my commitment to Rosie. I understood why she never wanted to get married again, but I wanted to make a statement to her that we were together forever. I want her to wear my ring and have my name. It was truly important to me.

Rosie strolled down the waterfront garden barefoot, as usual. She wrapped her arms around my chest from behind and snuggled her face in my back, under the floral wrapped pergola. She was breathtaking in her silky blush dress she had worn to supper at the Sailing Club. "You look beautiful, Love."

"Why thank you, Handsome," she responded with a smile. I felt her smile on the back of my dress shirt. I loved that smile, and I will never tire of hearing her call me that.

I turned to her, taking both of her hands in mine, and declared, "My Darling Rosie. I love ye more than I ever imagined. My love for you is infinite. I've been enamored with you since the first time I laid eyes on you. The first time you spoke to me in that adorable accent, you blew me away. Then you had that huge beamer and I knew we were fated for one another. I *knew* you fancied me." I confessed with a wink, smiling from ear to ear.

"After they took you from me, I was completely lost. I couldn't think clearly. I thought I lost you in the water, and my heart stopped beating. You are my best friend. You are my other half and you belong by my side for all eternity."

I cleared my throat got down on one knee.

"Here and now, I make this commitment to you. I, William Eoghan Henderson, will protect ye, love ye, honor, and cherish you forever. I will walk with you down every road, take every turn and faithfully be yours till the end of time. Will you do me the honor of accepting my commitment and being my partner in life?"

"Yes, oh yes, Liam! A thousand times, yes," She exclaimed, and knelt, wrapping her arms around my neck and kissed me as passionately as the first time. When she pulled away, she stayed knelt in front of me and took my hands. Smiling from ear to ear, and silently weeping, repeated my commitment to her.

"Here and now, I Rose Elizabeth Harris Kelly make my commitment to you. I will protect you, love you, honor, and cherish you forever. I will walk down every road and take every turn, faithfully by your side. You know I love you more than anything, Liam. You are my best friend and other half. I won't walk through life without you next to me." She leaned into me and I held her face in my hands. I kissed her with more passion than ever before. I didn't think kissing Rosie could get better, but it does every time. When we finished, I pulled her ring out of my pocket and placed it on her finger.

She held her hand up gazing at the ring on her beautiful hand for the longest time. After she finished remarking how beautiful the ring was and how well the oval cut diamond in the antique diamond-encrusted setting, complimented her hand she took it off. She turned it over and said, "You had my ring inscribed?"

"The engraving is wee and you don't have your reading glasses, so I'll tell you what it says."

I recited the inscription to her, "Rhea, goddess of my Universe." She reached up and pulled me down by my tie and kissed me passionately again and again. After several long minutes, she released me, saying,

"You know, I'll go shopping and buy you a ring. Would you wear my ring if I bought you one? I don't want any women thinking they can steal you away from me. I've been thinking about that for a while," she said with a smile.

"Aye, I'd be proud to wear your ring, Love. If you want a Commitment Ceremony for the girls to witness, you can have one. I'll gladly give you and the girls anything and everything. Will you take my name, Love?"

She looked up at me and smiled and said, "I adore you, Liam. I love being yours in every way. Besides, I've practiced writing it for ages." She giggled and beamed like a teenager.

Relief washed over me. I didn't think taking my name would be an argument, but I truly wanted it.

I stood and held out my hand to help her up. Smiling, I asked, "Would you dance with me please, Love?" She nodded, still smiling and I kept her hand, walking her to the deck, overlooking the Lough.

My life partner and I slow danced together and I serenaded her, as we continued laughing and kissing for half the night. "Since I'm on a roll, would you allow me to buy you a new motor? Your jeep is making an awful sound, and I worry with you being stranded about when it packs in."

"Today, you made me the happiest woman in the world. You get anything you want, Baby. I mean you did buy me the most beautiful diamond ring in Northern Ireland. Allowing you to buy me a newer ride is the least I could do, but whatever you choose, I prefer red," she suggested chuckling. "I am adding Mrs. into my name again too. I know we're not married on paper, Liam, but you are my husband in every way, and I intend on calling you that, as I am your wife.

Our commitment is stronger than the pen. It was written in our hearts." She declared placing her left palm on my heart.

"Mrs. William Henderson. That has a nice ring about it," I said grinning. My Love never stopped smiling all night. After carried my bride inside with our empty cocktails. "Darling, do you want a honeymoon?"

"Hell yeah," she exclaimed.

"Where do you want to go?"

"Surprise me," she said with a smile and a daring look in her eye.

"Alright, I plan on it. I'll be up in a minute," I said as she made her way upstairs to prepare for bed. I finished loading the dishwasher, but I had one more thing to do.

I still had to set Rosie's Commitment gift in place. I was already going to regardless of her answer. She deserved this. The Dutch Police finished their investigation of Grace and Rosie's kidnapping, omitting Kerberos' involvement. As a gift of our union, I had the painting professionally framed to match the decor of the Lough House. I hung the painting above the cut stone gas fireplace, as a surprise on our special day.

Stepping back my eyes observed the wall, checking the painting to see if I had centered it properly. Truly it was evident it had belonged there all along. I hadn't spent much time looking at it before, but I appreciated the painting as a work of art.

The painting was of a woman from the bust-up. She wore a plain blue dress that buttoned up to her neck. She had a white open banned collar. She faced most of the way to my left, but her head had yet to turn from me. She had fair skin, big round blue eyes, and a peachy cupid's bow. Her gaze

stuck to mine. Her blushed cheeks and almond-shaped face

suited her. What must have been long red hair was pinned at

the back in a large bun. The entire painting looked like it was

behind a slightly obscured glass window with a dull sheen.

She was looking through the glass at the viewer. No, I was

looking *at her* behind the obscured glass. It was only then, I

finally saw her.

*"Sweet Jesus, it's my Rosie."*

THE END

419

# Acknowledgments

With permission from the painting's owner, David N. Hart, the eldest son of Artist Nicolas Carone, the images of *The Woman Behind the Glass* were used in this novel. Any reproduction is prohibited.

Nicolas Carone (1917-2010)

I would like to thank my peer readers for their recommendations, my parents for their encouragement, and my children for allowing me time. I would also like to thank Erin Dooling (https://www.youtube.com/user/BeautyCreep) for her contribution of Scottish slang.

Thank you, Mrs. Mary Kay Loney and Mr. Martin Tierney for educating me in the art of the written word. Most importantly, I would like to thank Women's Aid Armagh Down for providing the glue, to piece ourselves back together.

# Resources

Women's Aid Northern Ireland 0808 802 1414
Womensaidarmaghdown.org.uk
Womensaid.org.uk

National Domestic Abuse Helpline 0808 2000 247
Nationaldahelpline.org.uk

Women's Aid Ireland
Womensaid.ie 1800 341 900

Scottish Women's Aid 0800 027 1234
sdafmh.org.uk

Printed in Great Britain
by Amazon

63435973R00253